THE
HEALINGS

THREE STORIES OF MIRACULOUS
HEALING FROM SCRIPTURE

LONNIE-SHARON WILLIAMS

WESTBOW
PRESS
A DIVISION OF THOMAS NELSON

ISBN: 978-1-4497-5799-1 (sc)
ISBN: 978-1-4497-5800-4 (e)

Library of Congress Control Number: 2012911633

WestBow Press books may be ordered through booksellers or by contacting:

WestBow Press
A Division of Thomas Nelson
1663 Liberty Drive
Bloomington, IN 47403
www.westbowpress.com
1-(866) 928-1240

Printed in the United States of America

WestBow Press rev. date: 07/16/2012

ACKNOWLEDGEMENTS

The Lord has blessed me to be able to write poems, plays and stories and it is through His hand on my pen that I began writing. So many people are to be commended for their generous time spent in helping me as I have tried to establish myself as a writer, especially Pastor Joyce J. McIntyre, who had the double job of being my muse and encourager. However, my first encouragers were my mother and father, the late Daisy and Robert Spivey, who have always told me to continue to write and to strive "to be the best writer you can be!" I also thank my sixth grade teacher, Mrs. Geneva Blackshear at Longwood Elementary in Cleveland, who felt I had the talent to write stories. I pray that I have lived up to all of their expectations.

To the many churches and schools that have allowed me to read my work and perform my plays during services and programs, I say thank you, thank you, thank you! You allowed me to publicly express my talent.

God bless and kudos to the Spivey family (Bobbie Jean, James, Lillian, Horace and Corky), as well as to the Sisterhood of Corrine Agrinsonis, Elizabeth Jefferson, Tracy McRae, Rachel Oden, Jonny Prell, Constance Sealey, Bernice Shaw, Hattie Smith, Elizabeth West, and Eve Young, all of whom were 'forced' to read, comment and critique my drafted stories; and to my publishing advisor, Amanda Parsons, who has to be commended for being so patient with me as I completed my stories.

A great big thank you to world traveler, G.F. Coyle III, who provided the cover picture for this book.

And finally, huge hugs and love to those who will read this book and consider the 'rest of the story' as written through my pen and computer.

Thank you Robert and Clare Graves for your patience, generosity and love!

I pray you will be enormously blessed!

THE HEALINGS

INTRODUCTION

As an avid reader of the Bible, I found myself wondering why the Lord did not give names to certain of the characters in the Bible. Jesus would stress "a certain man" instead of naming the man, or not giving names to the people He healed. I realized that some were of importance to the stories, while others only needed to be acknowledged.

For instance, Naaman the Syrian leper had an unnamed wife. What happened between the couple after his healing? What about the nameless leper who was healed with nine other men who returned to say thanks? No further information is written about him. There also was the nameless man who was healed by Jesus at the Pool at Bethzatha. What happened to him years later after Jesus told him to take up his mat and walk?

I tried to keep the stories consistent by naming the characters, giving them families and friends, and a bit of their history. It is always better to relate to them by adding a bit more information before and after their healings.

Hence, in the first story, Naaman's wife and the little maid now have names, friends and families. In the second, I continued the healed leper's story as he relates it to his daughter-in-law. The third story gives a bit more insight as to the character of the man who was healed by Jesus at the Pool of Bethzatha.

SHEERA
AND
COMMANDER NAAMAN

FROM 2 KINGS 5:1-20
A FICTIONAL BIBLE STORY

SHEERA AND
COMMANDER NAAMAN

Please note that this story is purely fictional, but taken from the Bible as related in Chapter 5 of Second Kings. The maiden that reported the ministry of the Prophet Elisha to Naaman's wife is unnamed in scripture, but I found it prudent to give her a name and a family. With the exception of recognizable historical figures, the characters, incidents and dialogues are products of my imagination only and are not to be construed as real or true. Any resemblance to actual events or persons, living or dead, is purely coincidental.

The Syrians were Semites who constantly waged war on the Israelites under the leadership of King Ben-Hadad II. The Syrians used raiders to keep them supplied with slaves for their mines and households. The raiders were noted for their brutality, but they also saved healthy captives to sell as slaves to the various nations for money and utilized the spoils of their raids for themselves.

Most of the names are fictitious and are not meant to resemble any character of the Bible, except the fact that scripture says Naaman was married and the young girl was taken as a slave from Israel from one of the raids (II Kings 5:2-4).

PROLOGUE

"It looks bad doesn't it, Amram? I can tell by the look in your eyes every time you bathe or dress me. I see your brows have been coming together quite often." He gave a small chuckle as he turned his head on the cloth pillow.

Commander Naaman had his back to his servant as he lay upon the wooden table. Amram, his personal valet-slave, made sure they were always alone when he took off his Master's armor and clothes. The small jars on the table contained herbs and a healing salve to keep the burning sensations at bay. His hands continued to rub the salves into his Master's back, but gave no comment.

After a while, he calmly stated, "At least the peelings have stopped for a while, my lord. It is good my mother gave me the recipe for this medicine before she died. It is doing its work by slowing the disease, but not great enough to stop the spread of it."

Amram had learned to school his features so that his Master would not realize how much he worried about the newly-formed boils. He had finished the front of the body and was now placing more herbs on the soft cloth and smoothed extra salve over the Commander's back, arms, hands, and now the back of the neck. He had been noticing how the boils were beginning to spread to the smaller parts of his Master's head, ears and fingers. Even the toes were developing small sores. He was aware that the smaller digits of the body would be the first to drop off. At least his Master still had feeling in those parts, which let him know they were not ready to begin the next stage.

The salve was also good to keep the insects away from his face. He used the herbs to slow the disease's progress and to try to eliminate the smell of rotting flesh, but even the Commander knew there was only so much the servant could do to slow the progression of the disease. Amram reached for the light robe and handed it to him.

The Commander slowly turned and looked at Amram with grateful eyes. "You are a good man, Amram, and your God must surely love you and your brother. Otherwise, I would worry more than normal about both of you catching this dreaded disease." He covered himself with the robe his servant offered him and tied the rope-like belt.

The Commander slid off the table to lace the sandals on his feet as he fixed a smile on his face. "How do I look? I don't want my wife to see me looking sad. She went today to offer more sacrifices to Rimmon, but our god has not answered my prayer or hers. Perhaps the prayers of you and your brother to your Israelite God will show more mercy."

Changing the subject, he said, "I'm feeling much better and will now go to the curtain, for I know Tirah is waiting for me. I don't want to be late for she worries so. You may go now to your own family. I will see you again in the morning."

Amram smiled as he bowed toward his Master. "I will be here early tomorrow, my lord, for the King has requested a meeting with you and your generals first thing in the morning. I know the Mistress will not keep you long, so after your visit you should go directly to bed. Your body needs all the rest it can get. General Meruru has sent word that he and the other generals will meet you by the palace walls first thing so that all of you may go into King Ben-Hadad's throne room together." After clearing the table and putting aside the small jars of medicine and herbs, the servant left the room.

Slowly Commander Naaman turned toward the room with the soft curtain at the door and entered to meet with his wife.

SHEERA AND COMMANDER NAAMAN

1

It was a beautiful day. Even though the sun was not yet above the horizon, the valley was a beautiful sight. There was the usual early morning hustle and bustle of people moving about. This small Samaritan village was hidden among small hills. The fertile land was thriving with crops throughout the land and there were fruits and vegetables for the inhabitants as the time of harvest slowly ended.

As the village awakened, the women fixed the grain and olive oil to begin making the day's meals. Their conversations included chattering about the last day of harvest, their husbands and sons, the little children and the upcoming harvest celebration once all the crops were finished harvesting. There was also a bit of gossip to share as the village became a buzz of voices.

The air was pungent with the smell of harvest. The crops of wheat were mostly stored and there was a sense of frivolity in the air. The men were doing what men usually do on a day such as this; and the women folk were doing what women usually do at this time of year. It was still early morning and the yellow ball in the sky had begun to rise. The sky was beginning to turn blue and clear, with hardly any clouds in the sky.

The morning air was balmy, the flowers were in bloom and there was an air of expectancy among the villagers.

But Sheera noticed none of this as she looked at the bushes and the men standing on large rocks by the trees. Lookouts were always on duty – day and night. The village had found favor with Yahweh and no attacks had taken place for some time. The Syrian raids had slowed down, of course, but the men did not want to be caught off guard. Even though the hills protected their small valley, the raiders were becoming bolder and had attacked a village within a three days' walk a few months ago. The smoke from the burning village could be seen from the hills.

No one knew what happened to the Israelites who survived the raiders' plundering. Young and old men who had tried to protect their village had spears and arrows in their bodies; the men who might have survived were not in sight. There were no chickens, sheep or other animals roaming around the area. Except for a few animals and human bodies strewn around, the village was deserted.

It was quickly noticed that very few men, women and children were among those who were left to bury their dead. The men from Sheera's village noticed this when they had gone to the burned out village. They viewed the devastation and began right away digging graves, for it was quickly noticed that the wild animals, birds, insects had begun to feast on the bodies.

The report the men gave on their return was not good.

2

Today was hunting day, and as the people began readying themselves, there was the wonderful smell of breakfast preparations. The men were sharpening their spears, arrows, and knives and were singing and praying for a large capture of meat. The younger women were readying their baskets to collect berries and grapes as the very young children played underfoot.

After eating and clearing their various cooking areas, the women began to prepare for their day, fixing cave and storage areas for any game that would be brought back by the males of the village. The men went off to hunt as the younger women headed for the woods, laughing and calling to each other as they walked with baskets on their heads, hips, and shoulders. There were plenty of berries and fruit to be picked, cleaned, and prepared for winter wine and jellies.

There was a good harvest this year of the corn, grain and wheat. Her father, Elah, had suggested rotating the wheat and grain so that other crops could be planted. He felt the soil was good for planting other fruits and vegetables and the traders would give the villagers new seeds from other villages and cities as they passed through their areas. He had recently been given small vines from a small fruit the traders called "strawberries" that grew above ground, but it would be two to three years before they would produce any fruit or the fruit would be ready for harvesting.

Ari smiled at Sheera as she collected berries from the bushes. He reached over and tried to help her, but Sheera pushed his hands away so she could reach the basket with one hand and collect berries with the other. Even though he was her best male friend, his laughter made her angry.

"Go away, Ari! You're bothering me. I'm going to be late getting back to the village!" She hurriedly tried to finish filling her baskets so she could begin the short walk back to the village, joining other girls her age who had also been collecting the various fruit that grew around the village.

She remembered when she was younger, the villagers would travel from one site to another as they needed food, pushing their chickens, sheep and cattle onward every six or seven months, but after finding this area, the men realized it was a good area for raising their families, animals, agriculture and safety. They had been living in this valley for at least four growing seasons.

Samaria had its problems, but their close-knit village was out of the way of raids and other dangers. Their grain and fruit grew plentiful, their animals reproduced healthy offspring, their chickens multiplied, and the small river and woods gave them their meat and fish; whereas, the mountains gave them wonderful sunrises and sunsets and protection from outsiders.

Ari left her and went to stand beside his little sister, Pridi, who had collected her berries near the riverbed. He waited as she struggled to tie her berry-laden scarf around her waist with her tiny hands. Always patient, he helped his sister tie the scarf, scooped her up and put her on his shoulders for the walk back to the village.

Taller than most of the young men his age in the village, Ari walked very straight, making sure his sister did not tilt with her burden. Pridi giggled as he walked sedately, screaming, "I'm too old to be on your shoulders, Ari!" Ari threw his head back and laughed loudly as she hit him on top of his head.

Sheera knew Ari liked her and that their parents would soon announce betrothal news to the villagers, even though she believed the people were already guessing about the upcoming announcement. The women would always smile knowingly at her when Ari came near her family's tent. She would have liked to have some say in the matter, but was pleased that her father chose Ari over some of the other young men.

She would accept the betrothal, not because she really wanted it, but because it was what her father desired for her and she was an obedient and diligent daughter. She loved her father above all other males and, besides, she and Ari were friends even though they could not wed for another three or four years, giving her time to accept the engagement. She was loved by his family, especially his little sister, Pridi, who thought of her as a big sister. Even her brothers had a kinship with his family, since Ari and Obid were best friends and little Amir's constant playmate was Pridi. Some of her female friends would have liked Ari to be their betrothed, but her father had discussed everything with Ari's father when the two were younger and the contract had been settled.

Little Amir had grown a little taller and was now allowed to go on the hunts with the older men. She hoped Amir would not be mistaken for an animal and thus receive an arrow through his leg or arm.

Yet, today she had a feeling of trepidation and sighed; it was unnerving for her to think of such things. What was wrong with her? She tried to concentrate on happy thoughts while she continued picking the last of the berries from the vines and bushes in her sight as she traveled back to the village.

Some of the young males had been left behind to watch over the women while the men went hunting and Ari was one chosen to do so. There were also a few others who were used as village keepers such as Ari, including Jeshua, Luti, Asrin, Jason and Shealtiel, also friends of her brother Obid. She did not know the others that well, but Ari was the one assigned to her section of the village. They rotated as security over the women and children, and Sheera knew that the next time Obid would be utilized for their area.

As she washed the berries in the cool water, her mind wandered to thinking about her village. It was good to be living in a place where everyone knew each other and she knew she was loved by her family and friends. There were other boys around her age that her father could have chosen, but Sheera never thought of them as prospective husbands. As young as she was, Sheera felt some were too immature for their age, and others had no brains to think of anything except themselves. She had heard a rumor that Shealtiel wanted to ask for her but when he learned Ari was to be betrothed to her, he left her alone. He was a good friend and likeable, but she favored Ari much more.

Picking up the last of her berries and scarf, she situated one basket on her left shoulder, and the smaller basket that held the grapes in the arc between her right arm and hip, and slowly walked toward the camp. Once again she sighed as she headed for her own home. She quickly prepared the afternoon meal and added some of the berries for dessert. Her father and brothers would soon be returning with the meat they had killed and she would help to dress the meat with the other women in the evening.

The village's men and boys had not returned by the time she had cooked the meal for her family and she constantly listened out for them. The men always came back with a large catch of fish and game and were noisy on their return from hunting. It was strangely quiet as they had not yet returned. As unease grew in her mind, she began to pray to Yahweh that whatever was bothering her would leave.

She had this same feeling when Amir was born. She knew before the midwife came from the birthing tent that her mother had passed away. The pregnancy was a hard one and her mother had not been well before she went into labor. She could still remember the chilling wail her father had given when he was finally allowed to go into the birthing tent to see his wife's still body. The baby lived, but his wife, Relana, did not. Sheera tried her best to comfort her father during his period of mourning, as well as help take care of the newborn. The midwife called for a wet nurse to help with Amir's care and the wet nurse gave her advice whenever she needed it.

Yahweh always came to her aid and calmed any fears she may have – why not now?

As the sun began to set, she heard the men returning. As always, they were laughing and thumping each other on the back. It seemed they had run into a flock of geese and decided to bring back as much meat as possible. Each man had a catch of at least five large fish and many ducks and geese hanging from a rope. The wild game was hanging by ropes from a tree limb and carried by two of the stronger men. Each of the smaller boys had a few fish and geese of various sizes on their ropes.

Small he might be, but Amir was also resourceful, strong for his age, and very intelligent. Sometimes Sheera would play a school game with him and Amir could quickly figure out the answers. When the traders came to the village, he always made a point of talking with them and could recite to the family word-for-word what they discussed. He had even picked up a few words in different languages from the traders as they passed through. Sheera was very proud of both of her brothers.

Obid was tall, muscular and a good fighter. He was one of the fastest runners in the village. And to Sheera, he was more handsome than his friends.

Little Amir called out to her trying to sound like his father, "Sheera, life is good and all is well!" She gave a smile to him as he approached, patting him on the arm as the men and boys headed for the areas where the meat would be processed for storage by the women.

Obid gave a large grin as he walked toward her with three large fish and two geese hanging on his rope. Little Amir had caught two fish, the larger of which her father later said was a fighter. Amir had help in bringing the fish toward shore, but as far as the small boy was concerned, he had caught the fish all by himself for it was on his line. She was happy to see everyone returning to the village in great spirits.

As they approached the village, the older men were singing a song the Prophet taught them at the last Passover sacrifice:

> Yahweh is great, Yahweh is good
> For His mercy endures to the end.
> Yahweh gives grace, mercy and hope,
> For life is good and all is well!

She thought to herself, "life *is* good and all *is* well." That is what her father, Elah, always said, and yet the same unease was still there.

That night, as she lay awake on her straw and fur pallet bed beside her little brother, she thought she felt the rumble of horses' hooves. She should have been asleep yet throughout the day, the eerie feeling would not subside that something fearsome was about to happen. So strong was this feeling that she did not undress for bed, but lay on top of her pallet and began to pray, "Oh, almighty Yahweh, be with us this day."

She felt whatever was to take place would happen soon.

3

Sheera could hear the thundering sound growing louder in the distance and hurried movements outside of the tent. She knew her father and older brother had also felt the rumblings and were pulling the furs and blankets off the tent doors.

She heard her father yell, "Get up, daughter, get up! The raiders are coming." Sheera quickly grabbed Amir and they began running, heading toward the hillside where caves had been prepared by the villagers in the event this would happen. Raiders from Syria and other nations were constantly burning villages, but theirs had always been avoided and left alone since Amir was born over four and a half years ago. The rumblings were too noisy and strong to be a few raiders, but by the drumming of horses' hooves, she knew there were many.

Amir, who was not fully awake, began to whimper and cry. "Hush, Amir. We must be quiet, so hush, hush!" It was hard to give comfort to him while running and when her own heart was beating as if her chest would open up and her heart would fall out.

They were almost to the hills when a large horse with a soldier came out of nowhere. "Ahhhh," cried her little brother as the rider swooped down and picked him up with one arm. Sheera continued to run as fast as her legs would carry her. As the rider continued racing onward, another arm picked her up and placed her body across a huge horse. "Amir," she cried, "Oh, Amir! Father! Obid!" she yelled as a hand closed over her mouth to stop her cries.

She watched as her friend, Ari, fell from a fierce blow to the head by the sword handle from one of the soldiers. Blood gushed from his skull as he lay beside a flaming tent. Sheera's legs were flailing wildly as she rode across the horn of the raider's saddle, but eventually she went limp when the soldier hit her on the back of her head and all was blackness.

4

Groggily, she slowly began to stir and saw her small village on fire; bodies were lying around the burned out tents and hovels, including Ari's. She saw many of the village's chickens and goats lying on the ground. The stench of death was everywhere. She did not know how long she had been unconscious, but it must have been for hours.

She watched as the raiders began herding the sheep in order to take them as plunder. The fish and game that was caught during the day lay across many of the soldiers' horses. She did not see her father or brothers and realized that the small army had devoured the living, including her family.

Sheera silently sobbed and prayed that her family's deaths were quick and that they were not lying somewhere with their life's blood slowly seeping out to later be eaten by the scavenging animals.

Her first lucid thought was that she would be raped by the soldier and either killed or left for dead, as had happened in other villages. She had only begun her 13th year although she was small for her age, and knew there was no hope for her. Women were not well treated during the raids by Syrians and other nations. Her head hurt so badly and eventually she lost consciousness again. When she awakened, she saw mountains and a small river below.

The soldier rode toward the raiders' camp near the mountains and almost threw her off his horse as he headed toward the campfire. Sheera was dragged by another soldier and then pushed by a large hand in the small of her back to enter into a large tent which had an odor of dead meat and blood and held other captive girls. There must be over 50 or so soldiers or raiders, she thought, as she went to the edge of the section that another soldier pointed out to her.

There was a lot of weeping and wailing by the many girls in the crowded tent – she counted at least 75 young girls from various villages as well as her own from the ages of 10 to 17 or 18. The languages of the girls were not only Hebrew, and she began to make out various dialects from other nations and clans but did not understand most. She did recognize one fact — fear was foremost in their whispers.

She could hear the soldiers talking outside the tent in Hebrew, Amalekite, Amorite and the Aramaic language as well as other languages, which she barely understood. She did, however, understand that they seemed to be discussing what to do with the girls. Some were throwing lots for certain of the girls and it seemed others wanted to sell them to foreigners for the money they could bring.

Eventually, a tall, thin but muscular man in uniform stepped into the area and the bargaining stopped. He began barking orders at the raiders. Guards were then placed around the tent as other soldiers began to bed down for the night.

The girls realized he was a high-ranking soldier who had not been with the raiders. As he barked orders, a group of soldiers came to walk them to an area where they were able to relieve themselves and brought them back to the tent.

Upon their return, each girl began to lie down on the dirt floor of the tent, some having younger girls lying next to them. Sheera could see that many were sisters or cousins and they tended to huddle together in fear before allowing themselves to sleep. She did not see many girls from her village, but a few of the older ones stayed together.

She sat down beside one of the nearest poles which held the tent upright, and putting her back against the pole began to fall asleep from fatigue. As her head fell forward, her last thought was of her family. Poor Amir, poor Obid, she thought as a tear slowly fell down her cheek before falling asleep. Her father was more than likely dead also. She knew there was no hope for Ari for blood from the head and mouth were sure signs that he was dead.

5

The sun was barely up when a group of soldiers lined up the girls and took them to the small river that was down a short hill near the camp. The girls quickly took turns relieving themselves and washing up while the others watched for the soldiers. They did not want to strip off their clothes, but used their scarves as washcloths to wash away dirt and bloodstains where some had fallen or been hit by the soldiers.

One big and muscular raider came near and grabbed one of the young 15 or 16 year old girls who screamed loudly. As he began to drag her toward the high bushes, he slapped her to quiet her screams. As her unconscious head lolled from side to side, some of the other girls began running from the river, screaming and even tried to attack the man. Still dragging her, the raider kept one big burly hand on the captive girl's arms while trying to fight off the others with his other hand. The girls continued screaming loudly.

Out of no where, the large lead officer stood in front of the raider and slammed his fist into the man's face. The raider released the unconscious girl, who fell to the ground. The other girls helped to carry the girl back to the side and began to wipe her face with cool water.

The raider stared at the leader in a defiant stance and put his hands on his hips as he cursed the leader. The leader said something in response to the raider, then grabbed him by the neck, lifting his feet from the ground and cursing spewed from his mouth. Even though the girls did not know what was said, they knew it was nothing good!

Something in the hand of the leader gleamed in the sunlight before the raider slid slowly to the ground in a dead heap. Silently, two other raiders came from behind their leader, picked up the dead man to carry him away. A long knife was sticking out of the man's chest as they grabbed his arms and legs and carried him behind the same bushes he had planned to drag the young girl.

The commanding officer turned toward the quieted girls, bowed and said something in a pseudo-Hebrew language, that all understood to mean they would not be touched by any of the men. One of the men who carried the dead raider came and handed the leader his cleaned-off knife. The leader looked at the knife and returned it to the empty leather sheaf on his hip. He again bowed to them and went back to where he came from on the other side of the tall bushes.

Strangely, it seemed the soldiers had all been given orders by their commanding officer to not touch the girls unless there was a problem. Sheera knew at this point that these were not just Syrian raiders, but a mixture of tribes and nations who raided villages for the spoils. Even their uniforms were not the same, but possibly uniforms from soldiers they had killed. They had probably been without a woman for some time and the now dead raider had decided to use one of the girls for his own pleasure. His death was a lesson to the others.

The girls went back to the river, finished their ablutions and they continued their trek to their unknown destination. The young girl who was grabbed was now awake and still fearful of the raiders, but she was situated to walk in the middle of other girls her age.

One of the younger girls had scraped and bruised hands and knees because she had tried to crawl to safety when her village was plundered. Sheera could see the girl was bruised and sore and took off her girdled scarf to wash the younger girl's knees. She looked to be about 11 or 12 years of age, and even though she did not speak in a Samaritan dialect, they were still able to communicate. She was an Israelite, but her dialect varied from Sheera's. She told Sheera her name was Risa from an area near Shechem. They stayed together after that, sleeping, eating and walking beside each other.

The bleating of sheep and lowing of cattle was behind the tent informing the girls that most of their villages' animals had been spared. A few of the sheep and cattle had been killed during the night and were roasting on spits as food for the soldiers and some were to be shared by the men and girls.

Later, during one of their stops, the soldiers gave the girls strips of roasted meat, dried figs, stale bread to eat and water to drink and using hand signals and various languages told them to eat quickly and be ready to walk. The girls lined up behind the horses and in front of the foot soldiers and slowly walked toward the rising sun. They had to endure the long walk, but also stepped around the horses' waste, and the men's cursing and prodding.

Every once in a while, throughout the day the soldiers would stop and rest the girls, but eventually they continued the trek, with Sheera and Risa walking side by side. The herded animals were far behind with men allowing the beasts to slowly walk toward their destination.

6

On the fifth day, the heat was unbearable. It seemed there was no sunrise; the sun just stayed in the same place all day. The girls were tired and wanted to rest, but their rest times were becoming fewer and far between. Some were so parched, their lips seemed to stick together. They were afraid to breathe through their noses because of the insects which would fly into their mouths.

Soon the leader called a halt beside a small stream. The stop was not for the girls or the raiders, but because the herded animals were braying and bleating for they were also exhausted. The herders ran to the leader and complained so the leader was required to stop for a rest. The girls literally dropped to the ground with fatigue. When the water buckets were distributed among the groups, some of it splashed down the fronts of their clothes in their rush to drink.

Once again they began walking, when one of the older girls bent low, sneaking around the groups of girls, and escaped from the line in an attempt to run away. She had not gone more than 10 meters, when one of the soldiers turned and saw her; then laughing, hurled a spear which went through her back with the sharp end coming out through her chest. As the spear went through, she gave a pitiful and haunting cry and slumped to the ground. The line of girls gasped and covered their mouths so as to not cry out, but continued walking, many silently crying.

No one said anything – not the girls, or the soldiers or the commanding officer, who saw everything. Did the girl think she would be raped by the raiders, or just wanted to run away from them? Sheera felt there was no reason for the foolish girl to try to run – where would she go? No one even knew where they were or where they were going. They were in a desert area and the only water they were given came from the raiders.

The soldiers and girls traveled in this manner for a few more days, yet because of the one runaway, no one else tried to escape. Their captives did not even put ropes on them, just prodded them with their spears to keep them on the move. The girls were only allowed to stop to relieve themselves or to eat a meager meal of grapes, dates or figs and hard bread and water. The soldiers had finished the roasted meat and it did not look as if they would be roasting any more. Far behind them they could see the few men still herding the other animals.

One night the fish the men from her village had caught was placed in front of them, but few ate the meal. What they didn't eat, the soldiers divided among themselves. Each night, the soldiers set up the same foul-smelling tent and the girls were again herded inside to sleep. After traveling in this fashion, the girls were usually so fatigued they would quickly fall asleep, only to be awakened early the next day, meagerly fed, and pushed onward.

Even though Sheera had previously guessed, one night the other girls began talking among themselves that these men were not regular Syrian soldiers but raiders. One evening as they discussed this fact, one of the raiders came to the tent's opening and began yelling and, using hand signals, told them to be quiet and go to sleep.

These were the type of men who plundered villages for other nations to make money from slaves and rustle animals. Many nations only fought for land or plunder, but raiders were made up of men from various nations, mostly outlaws to supply slaves to other nations to make whatever money, jewels, or gold they could get.

7

For what seemed like weeks, the men and girls finally came to a large city. There was a walled fort, a few larger houses near the fort and on the outskirts, which Sheera understood them to be the homes of the well-to-do, and a larger building which she believed to be the palace.

As their captors brought them to the middle of the walled city, they were told to line up. Risa began whimpering so Sheera put her arm around her and tried to shush her. One of the soldiers grabbed Risa by the upper arm and dragged her out of the line. A man standing on the sidelines came forward and began gesturing for her to turn around, checking her mouth, legs and back, and began bartering with the soldier.

Sheera looked down the line and saw other girls being pulled forward and foreigners coming to haggle prices for the girls. Slaves, she thought, we're going to be slaves! An older girl communicated to her that they would either become slaves, concubines or whores. The worst was being a whore for the soldiers. She said she was praying for slavery.

As Sheera was pulled out of the line, she saw a beautiful woman on the sidelines of the slave area and looked at her beseechingly. "Please, Lord," she prayed, "let the woman come to buy me – not a soldier or any man." About that time, a lecherous looking Syrian man was looking Sheera over, feeling her shoulders, breasts, and arms and sliding his hands around her buttocks. She felt the hair on her arms rise up. "Oh, no, not him! Please Yahweh, help me!" She closed her eyes and began praying.

As she opened her eyes, the woman's eyes locked with hers. The woman gestured toward a soldier who pulled her from the slave block away from the Syrian man and brought her to the woman, making Sheera turn around for viewing. Three others were also brought to stand in front of her.

The Syrian man started to complain that he was looking at the girl first, but the soldier pointed to the woman and he stopped speaking and went back to the slave block to look at other young girls. She could tell he was angry, but the soldier pointed at him to return to the other slaves.

The woman softly spoke to them in a Hebrew tongue. "Are you from Samaria in Israel, Baal-Shalishah, Gilgal, or Sidon?" she asked.

"I am an Israelite from Samaria," Sheera quietly replied keeping her eyes toward the ground as she saw the other slaves doing. Two of the girls replied in kind and the third girl looked confused, but gave her name as Shatii.

Money was quickly transferred from one hand to another from a man she presumed was the woman's high-ranking servant who came with her. She had been purchased by the pretty woman. Sheera realized she had hardly breathed until she was purchased. She noticed that Shatii still looked afraid, so she put her arm around her and the girl tremulously returned her smile. Shatii was not an Israelite and was unable to understand what had just happened.

Soon, other slaves were purchased by the same woman and again money exchanged hands from the woman's servant, as the soldier gave the woman a wide smile and bowed before her. The woman acknowledged the soldier's smile and turning, gave a signal. The woman's servant and another soldier came forward to put a dark band around Sheera's arm, the other girls' arms, as well as the two young men who had also been purchased by the woman.

The high-ranking servant turned to the woman and both talked quietly together. The woman seemed to be giving him instructions and when she was finished he bowed to her. At this point Sheera realized even though he was a servant – he was one the woman respected and trusted. He went to the young men and spoke to them in another language. Both of the men nodded their heads signifying that they understood what he was saying.

As she finished watching the placing of the bands on the newly purchased slaves, the woman explained, "The band shows that you have been purchased by me. You will all receive another band when you enter my household. I do not believe in branding my servants, although many still follow that custom."

Sheera looked at the band and then the woman, who explained, "I need more workers for the household. You and the three girls behind you will remain with me, but the others will be used throughout the compound." She looked into Sheera's face and put her hands on both of her cheeks. "My last maid passed away and my husband sent me to purchase another. You are young but I think you will do nicely."

Sheera was surprised; the woman did not say "slave" – she said "maid." The woman turned and spoke in Aramaic to the servant standing regally next to her. The man nodded his head, faced the newly purchased slaves, and then spoke to each of the groups in their native languages, explaining that if they decide to run away until they get to their destination, they will be caught and killed. All looked toward the man with something akin to fear, but when he finished speaking, he smiled warmly at them.

Once again, he and the woman communicated in Aramaic and Sheera recognized some of the words. She believed he was saying that all was in readiness at the house. The servant bowed his head and left the group. He walked toward the lead carrier and said something to him. The lead carrier bearer answered in the affirmative to whatever question was asked and went to the stand at his post.

The woman gave another signal and the lead carrier and three muscular men came toward them. The carrier was brought to the woman and lowered; after the woman climbed into it, it was lifted. The soldier who sold Sheera to the woman signaled to her she should walk behind the men. Sheera kept her head down when she saw the other purchased slaves do so and followed behind the carrier along with the three girls from her group, as well as two young boys. The young men who were purchased followed behind the woman's servant, but traveled a different way.

Sheera chanced to look around in the event her family might be on the slave block, but there was no sign of them.

8

Slowly the group made their way through the crowded center of town. People stepped back to make way for the carrier and its followers and Sheera realized this was a woman of wealth and honor.

As they walked, once again, she thought of her baby brother, Amir. Their mother died giving birth to Amir and her father did his best to raise his three children. The village women were helpful to a man with a newborn and two other children. There were also women who wanted to be the new mother to Elah's children, but Elah said he only loved one woman.

Although Sheera was young, her father taught her many things and though small, she had the intellect of a grown woman. The female relatives and the women of the village taught her about herbs and medicines, cooking and cleaning; a male cousin taught her to fish and hunt, and others taught her about life outside of their village.

Another carrier was moving toward them and she knew that the carrier was heading for the slave block. As they passed, the women inside both carriers smiled and waved at one another – they must pass by each other often, she thought. There were four bearers for this carrier also and one of the young men holding the passing carrier looked at Sheera and as her eyes met his, he gave her a quick wink. Blushing, she put her head back down and continued walking behind the other slaves.

Sheera prayed that her life would not be one of ill treatment. The woman who purchased her was beautiful, but possessed the very sad eyes for someone who seemed to have wealth as well as sorrow.

Silently she gave thanks to Yahweh that she was not purchased by the lecherous-looking Syrian or a soldier and asked that He be with her; and if her family was still alive to be with them also. She prayed that Risa and the other girls would be well treated by whomever purchased them.

As she prayed, she was grateful that her father made sure his family knew of the One True God whom they worshipped. The High Prophet, Elisha, would pass through their village and when he arrived, there were always special offerings, sacrifices, and festivities. Yahweh is a good God, she thought. Elisha taught them how Yahweh loved the Israelites and that no matter what happened, they would always be in His heart.

Elisha explained how they were brought out of Egypt through the Prophet Moses. He stressed that the Lord was always with them, even when they did wrong. He told them their history, about the plagues that were sent by Yahweh in order to release them from Egyptian bondage, the cloud and the pillar of fire which constantly led them through the wilderness and the desert, and how the land they occupied had been called the Promised Land. Their patriarchs, Abraham, Isaac and Jacob had lived in the Promised Land. It was the land given to them by God for his people. She hoped Yahweh would always remember her and her family -- whether they lived or died, even if they were no longer in Samaria.

Sheera was not ignorant of the Syrian way of life, having listened to the traders that passed through the village, but knew they did not worship Yahweh. Amir had told them many stories of the Syrians from listening to the traders, who also had problems with raiders. She wondered which gods the Syrians worshipped. She had heard of Rimmon, one of the chief Syrian gods that accepted animal as well as human sacrifices, but knew they also worshipped other lesser gods. I will not bow down to their gods and idols, she vowed. Only Yahweh is God!

Soon, the group came to a small palace near the fortress wall. The carrier was lowered and the woman alighted from the curtained area of the carrier and went into the front of the palace. One of the strong men who carried the woman motioned for Sheera and the other girls to follow them. The girls all grouped together and were led to the back of the house, which presumably was the slaves' wing. She understood that this was where she would probably be staying. The men walked away, this time motioning for the young men to continue to follow them. The young males headed to where she could hear chickens, pigs, cattle, and whinnying horses and thought the young men might be working in the stable area.

The four girls met with other female slaves and were divided by an eunuch and she and the others were given light-weight tan gowns to put on. At first she started to balk at putting on Syrian wear, but looked at herself and realized her clothing was filthy. None of the girls had been allowed to truly bathe and were wearing the same clothing they had on from their respective raided villages.

Groups of women speaking different languages came and took them to a pool in the back and gestured for them to bathe and put on the clothes they had been given.

The girls were helped to undress and go into the pool. There were curtains around the area and the slaves gave them a cloth with oils and a small pumice stone to wash the dirt and grit away. All had lye soap and scrubbed themselves slowly, then vigorously as they realized that now they could wash their hair and bodies without soldiers looking on. No one said anything as they finished bathing, drying themselves and reached for the towels that were being offered.

After dressing, the new slaves were then led to the side of the house and told to sit in a small room. Here, they were given a small chunk of goat cheese, a bowl of warm gruel made of wheat and sweetened with honey, dates and nuts, a chunk of coarse dark bread and cool water. Being hungry, the girls were grateful for something that really tasted like a decent meal.

9

The pretty lady from the carrier came from behind a group of curtains and motioned for them to stay seated. A tall stool was by the entrance and the pretty lady sat as a young girl came out, stood beside her, and began interpreting in various languages what the pretty lady was saying. They were to become maids for the lady and Sheera had been picked to be her personal maid. Sheera would be sleeping with the same three girls for now, but would be moved later once she learned her duties. She would be working in the same area as the pretty lady, who was introduced as Mistress Tirah. She would be dressing and attending her and serving her only.

After giving a few final instructions, the pretty lady left the girls with the interpreter. The interpreter's name was Aweh, who explained that any questions Sheera and the others had should be asked of her so that there would be no error in what duties they were to perform.

Aweh explained that all of the maids would be well treated as long as they obeyed what they were told and do what should be done within the household. Mistress Tirah had a husband by the name of Commander Naaman, a well respected leader in the Syrian army, who reported directly to the King. She stressed that Naaman was a good leader and had many men under him, but would not always be seen by them as he was a leader in their wars and performed a lot of personal duties under the command of the King.

Sheera asked Aweh how she came to speak Hebrew and other languages, and the young woman replied she was taken with her family during a raid. She was still young, approximately three, perhaps four. Her village had been plundered and she barely remembers her family. She was well treated and stayed with other slaves until reaching the age of 7 or 8. By that time she had learned approximately five different languages from listening to the household slaves, the traders and the soldiers who passed through the area.

Because she could quickly learn languages, she later became an interpreter for the household. She had since learned about 15 languages and dialects – some of which she seldom used. Most of the captured people spoke many different languages and she was able to make everything easier for the household by working with the servants. Aweh looked to be approximately 13 or 14, but seemed much older than her years. She was very pretty and had a soft voice.

She informed the group that she, too, was a servant, but a personal servant only to Mistress Tirah. She was well liked by the other servants because she was able to settle arguments and explain Syrian customs to the new ones. Though a servant and wearing servants' clothing, she was dressed in a different lighter color from the other servants.

Sheera was later allowed to sit and talk alone with her and mentioned she was surprised that she and the other girls were not called "slave" but "maid." Aweh's eyes began to water a little and turned her head as she explained that the last personal maid had been a friend of hers, but caught a disease of the lungs and died. She could not breathe often, but the Mistress did not hold her coughing spells against her when she was unable to fulfill all of her duties. The maid finally passed away during the night about two full moons ago after a long bout of wheezing.

"You will be replacing Leda, who was a good maid, obedient, and never gave the mistress any problems," she explained. "The mistress mourned for her for such a long time that her husband suggested she should go to the slave marketplace and get another young maiden. You see, her husband cannot give her children so she loved Leda as her own. She had hair and coloring similar to yours for Leda was about your age and build, you see."

Aweh showed Sheera where she would sleep after her training and explained she would work with Sheera for a few days to get her accustomed to her duties.

"Mistress Tirah is a good woman and treats all of her servants very well. She will not have you beaten unless you do something really terrible, or try to run away or steal something," she warned her. "All slaves in this city are not so well treated."

Aweh took her to another room where a meal had been prepared and Sheera met up with the same three girls who arrived in the house with her. They became quick friends and were named Pua, Aleea, and Shatii. Shatii was from Sidon and did not talk much, but Pua, Aleea and Sheera quickly became good friends for they were all from Samaria and they had no problem communicating. Using their hands to gesture, they were able to also discuss many things with Shatii until eventually all learned Aramaic.

Aweh then left after explaining to the other girls that soon Sheera would be sleeping in a room she had earlier been shown near Mistress Tirah's living quarters. The three other maids would be in another area farther down a long hall, but all would take their meals in the same room. Aweh would meet with all the other maids in the morning to begin their training in the many duties to be performed for Mistress Tirah and the household. The girls would also be schooled in the Syrian language and their way of life.

10

As all the new girls ate together, they began discussing their capture and one reported that most of them had been given good treatment, considering the long walk. All were sorrowful because they did not know where their families were, or even if they were still alive. Sheera mentioned her brothers and father and wondered if they were still alive, made slaves, or if they had been killed in the fighting. She wondered what happened to Risa, the friend she made during their walk to Damascus. They all discussed what they had left behind in their villages and clans. No one mentioned the girl who tried to run away.

One of the girls said she was told by other servants that some of the captured men were led away to the caves where they would be mining for gold and silver, along with some of the older boys who had also been captured. Many would be working in the fields and some would take care of the animals like the two young men who were purchased at the same time as they by the Mistress.

Some of the men who had shepherding skills would work as shepherds. Others who were too old to do any work were taken away, but no one knew where. They all figured they were either put to death or would be used in pagan sacrifices to the Syrian god, Rimmon. No one was sure of this information.

Another said she heard that some of the older girls were sold to old Syrian men, some to soldiers for a few pennies, and others would probably become whores. The lucky ones would become concubines in wealthy households. All realized they were only speculating from what had been told to them in their villages.

The girls finished their meals and were wondering what to do with their eating utensils and bowls when an older woman silently came to take them away. The woman did not say anything, but Sheera noticed her eyes were very alert as she tidied the area. The older woman quickly looked the girls over and her eyes rested on Sheera. She gave a slight smile as she nodded her head towards them and her smile grew wider as Sheera returned the smile. The woman's eyes discreetly studied Sheera for a short while before leaving the area.

The girls soon decided they had better get some sleep because Aweh had said she would come to get them early in the morning. It was a long time before Sheera fell asleep. All she could think about was her family. She just wished she had some word as to whether her father and brothers were alive or dead, realizing it was not knowing that made her cry before falling asleep.

Daily Aweh made all the new captives rise before the sun was up. She held a small school, teaching Sheera and other captives the Syrian language of Aramaic for a few hours. Later, she instructed the new maids for Mistress Tirah on how they would be serving her.

Aweh gave them various instructions and said there were three main rules for all slaves. She advised them not to try escaping because they would be killed when caught; they could not fraternize with the male slaves without permission, and no one was to enter the curtained area in the rear of the house. Even though Mistress Tirah called them maids, they were still slaves of Commander Naaman, the Master and husband.

11

Sheera had never seen Master Naaman and had no intention of running away. There was evidence that there was a Master, but he had never made his presence known. The memory of the young girl with the spear through her back was a constant reminder of what happens to runaways. None of the soldiers had bothered to stop to bury her or put dirt or rocks on top of her body and knew the carrion birds had finished her remains within days.

Aweh had given tours to all the maids and informed each of them where to report each morning. Sheera would report only to the Mistress and her duties were to clean the areas where Mistress Tirah resided, be of service when she entertained, take care of her clothing and make sure the Mistress was comfortable. She was instructed to never venture into certain areas around the compound, and the Mistress would give her any other instructions or duties. It did not take her long to learn her duties for the Mistress.

As far as she knew, only Mistress Tirah went every night into the curtained area. However, after she came out, Sheera would hear the Mistress softly crying. She felt it incumbent to not ask questions, but she wondered what took place within the curtained room.

As a fast learner, the language was not too confusing, and Sheera's duties were very simple – cleaning the various areas of the house, escorting the Mistress when she left the area, walking beside the carrier in the streets of the city, carrying packages, setting out food for the Mistress and sometimes Aweh and, on occasion, standing behind the Mistress to fan her during the heat of the day.

Sheera had a lot of free time during the day, which was unusual for a slave, and there were times when she would go to the kitchen area with the women who were over the meals and help with the cooking when the Mistress entertained.

Since she was used to cooking for her father and brothers, this was the work she really enjoyed. Whenever she quickly finished her work, she would run to the kitchen area and help out until she was summoned by the Mistress, who knew she enjoyed it and would not call for her unless there was an urgent duty to be performed.

Mistress Tirah noticed and reported to Aweh that Sheera was very adept with her hands. Aweh saw that Sheera liked to work with her hands and requested that the Mistress allow her to learn to spin fine wool and linen in the spinning room with the older women. Sheera was taught by Aweh and another spinner, catching on quickly and was allowed to use the leftover materials to make outfits for herself and for the other maids.

The cloth was very fine because of the methods used by the Syrian clothiers and tailors. Her clothes at home were very coarse, but until she worked with the clothiers she had never known it – for in her village, everyone pretty much dressed the same. When the traders came, if there was enough animals or fur to barter, her father had on occasion treated his daughter by purchasing a few fancy scarves. The scarf she had on during the Syrian raid was the only piece of home since her capture and she treasured it. She had washed away the blood stains from Risa and kept it cleaned and folded in her small personal box until she was ready to wear it.

The scarf was the last article her father had purchased prior to the raid and she wore it as a girdle, making sure it was always clean. The rest of her village clothes had disappeared after she was brought to the compound and, she thought, possibly burned.

She noticed that the women servants in the compound wore sandals. Not the same type as the Mistress, but a flat bottom with lacing on top. It had taken Sheera some time to get used to the sandals for in her village no one wore shoes of any type. She was a slave and even she knew that slaves did not wear shoes. They were always barefoot to show their rank. However, Mistress Tirah's personal maids had a better grade of sandals and after a time she began to enjoy wearing the sandals for she no longer had small stones to take from between her toes.

12

Within a few months, Sheera had honed her duties and skills to the satisfaction of Aweh and Mistress Tirah. She enjoyed seeing Mistress Tirah smile, even though the smiles never really reached her eyes. There was a certain sadness about her, even though she had everything a woman in her position enjoyed. She was always sad in the evenings, especially after returning from behind the curtained room.

Once, when she tried to question Aweh about it, she noticed the girl never really answered her questions. It did not take her long to realize that Aweh kept the Mistress' secrets; therefore Sheera tried to keep her many questions to herself.

When Sheera had her first monthly, it was Mistress Tirah and Aweh who took care of her, explaining the courses of women and how to stay hygienically clean. Sheera knew some things about her own body functions from listening to the women of her tribe when she was growing up. She also knew that when her courses began she should have been hidden away in a special tent area, but the Syrians did not follow the laws of Moses. However, the Israelite women in the kitchens advised her to never come into the kitchens for seven days and she noticed that during those times, Aweh would also lessen her duties around the Mistress.

13

The years swiftly passed and one afternoon the Mistress left the house along with two of the other maids as escorts, leaving Sheera alone to finish a duty in the kitchen. Coming from the kitchen that evening through the long hall, Sheera noticed the curtains to the small room had been pushed aside. She headed toward the curtains to straighten them back into place, and came face to face with a very tall man who was trying to straighten the curtains from inside the room.

As they stared at each other, Sheera quickly realized this must be the Master. He was in full regalia – holding a shield with strange Syrian symbols, a coat of arms with similar markings, as well as a metal helmet and girdle.

"I'm sorry, sir," she stammered in Aramaic. "I did not know you were there. I was trying to rearrange the curtains which had come apart. It will not happen again." Totally frightened, she knew she had disobeyed Aweh's instructions.

"Quite all right," he answered in Hebrew and smiled at her. He studied her for a moment, and then spoke in a calm, resonant voice, "You must be Sheera, my wife's new maid. You've been here for quite some time but this is the first I've seen you; I almost thought I saw a ghost. You look so much like Leda. I am Naaman, commander of King Ben-Hadad's army, and husband to your mistress. Do not be afraid; I will not report you. My wife is very pleased with you. Let's keep it that way, hmmm?"

Sheera noticed the small white boils on his face which was not covered by his helmet, and the bluish color of his hands where his skin had partially peeled itself. She could barely see his face through the helmet, but it was very noticeable to her. The helmet hid a lot, but she recognized the peeling skin as the dreaded disease known as leprosy. "Thank you, sir," she quietly whispered.

Turning on her heels she proceeded to leave the area and when she was out of sight of the Master, she ran to her own room. Israelites with sores and boils such as his were never allowed inside the house and were kept to the outside areas of the town; most of them isolated themselves by living in caves or makeshift abodes, keeping to the Law of Moses.

When the lepers came to get water, they used special well areas not those located in the center of the village; and to get food from their families, they were required to yell "unclean, unclean" before coming near the townspeople. There were times when even the family would have nothing to do with a leprous relative. She found it strange that this Syrian leper was allowed to roam the house.

Slowly it dawned on her that the reason Mistress Tirah would never have any children was because she could not come too close to her husband – for he was a leper. She was only able to have private meetings with him and be separated by a curtain. She decided to keep this information to herself. It would not do to speak of it and let others become aware that she knew of the Master's disease — or how she knew.

14

Later that evening, after serving her Mistress, Aweh asked Sheera to eat her meal with her in her personal quarters. Sheera knew she was in trouble and planned to tell her side of the story because she did not want to be whipped for disobedience or sold to the soldiers.

Aweh saw the fear in her eyes and told her she had no reason to be afraid. She only wanted to find out how Sheera was doing and to give her some private language lessons. Still Sheera was afraid for Aweh had never before asked her to eat in her separate quarters, which was located on the other side of the hall behind the Mistress' rooms. In fact, she had never even seen Aweh's quarters for she did not have to share with other slaves.

The other girls were surprised that Sheera would not be eating the evening meal with them and when Aweh arrived, Sheera followed her out of their small eating room and went through a long hallway to Aweh's living quarters which, to her, were luxurious.

The main room had a small brazier in the middle on which she could do her own cooking if she desired, but was also used to keep the area warm in the cool evenings.

The small table was set for two as she beckoned Sheera to have a seat. There was a bed pallet, with lots of pillows, and curtains which hid her bath and another section which hid her chamber pot. On the floor was clean straw along with small idols and candles in a circle, which gave off a relaxing amount of light. Sheera looked around and tried not to admire the room by gawking. Her area was not as elite, although comfortable for her needs.

She was not surprised to see the idols and the candles, but said nothing. Aweh was not an Israelite, so she probably worshipped another god. Perhaps the Syrian god, Rimmon, or another pagan deity in the many temples scattered throughout the area.

The same older woman who brought food to her quarters came in with food for the two of them, but the meal was more lavish. Again, the woman studied Sheera, smiling at her while keeping her eyes to the floor as she served the meal. After the servant left the room, Aweh explained that her meals came from the Mistress' own table.

She and Mistress Tirah had become close friends over the years because of her husband's ailment. As she told this to Sheera, Aweh lifted an eyebrow at her knowingly. She knew Sheera had questions about the Master and the Mistress. It did not take Sheera long to realize that Aweh knew of her meeting with the Master and was waiting to hear what she would tell.

As they ate the tasty food, both girls idly chatted about the house, the gardens and the surrounding areas, the other slave girls and their duties. Finally, they discussed Mistress Tirah. Sheera cautiously explained what happened that afternoon and how she finally met Master Naaman.

Aweh listened but did not ask any questions or chastise her. Noting that the younger girl had finished eating, after wiping her mouth Aweh stood up and moved to a corner of the room where there were two small benches and, indicating one of them to her, both sat down facing one another.

Aweh took Sheera's hands in hers and began to explain the history of Naaman and his wife: Tirah had been promised to Naaman at an early age. Tirah was happy about the betrothal because Naaman, although five years older, was a handsome up and coming young soldier in the King's army, following in the footsteps of his late father. Because of his successful campaigns in war, he quickly rose up the ranks and soon became a commander. He was dearly loved by the king as if he was one of the king's royal sons. In fact, when the king went to worship in the temple of his god, Rimmon, it was often Naaman's arm the King leaned upon if the King's other sons or valet was not available.

However, two or three years after their marriage, Naaman began to have rashes and soon broke out in small sores, which later was shown to be leprosy. Because of the betrothal agreement, Tirah did not have to remain his wife, but she refused. As the sores grew and his body became waxy and began to peel, it was agreed that they could no longer live as husband and wife in the normal sense. Yet, both agreed to not be separated, and chose to live in the same house.

Mistress Tirah visits her husband every evening behind the curtains because he refused to let anyone but his wife see him. Naaman has loyal soldiers and servants who see to his daily needs and never leave his side, even in combat. But each night when he is not in combat, he still comes to speak with his wife behind the curtains. Both knew there would never be any children from their union, but they still love each other.

"A few of Naaman's personal servants are from the Israelite regions. Those servants know of your religious laws against touching lepers, but these Israelites have sworn to stay beside him. They do touch, bathe and dress him, and your God has never inflicted them with the disease."

"Because he is a good Master, Naaman has never worried whether those servants would do him any harm. His soldiers are also very loyal and when he has episodes — such as peelings and burning sensations due to his illness — the soldiers allow only the Commander's personal servants to attend him. When that happens, he refuses to let the Mistress visit with him."

When Mistress Tirah went to purchase a new maid and saw Sheera, she immediately thought of her last maid. "You look a bit like her," Aweh confided to her. "You're about her size and coloring. Leda was an Israelite also, but was always sickly, whereas you are healthy. Mistress took care of her as a mother would take care of her own child. Take care that you do nothing to distress her," she warned her.

Sheera said she had been noticing how sad Mistress Tirah would become whenever she came from behind the curtains. She wished there was some way she could help her, yet in Israel, all lepers stayed outside the areas of the city, following the laws of Moses in connection with cleanliness. Aweh pointed out that those were Israelite religious laws, not Syrian laws.

Sheera explained to Aweh the Israelite religion, how her nation follows the rules and laws of their father Abraham and Moses. She explained her Jewish heritage and the laws of cleanliness as her father had explained it to her from her childhood.

When she mentioned Yahweh, Aweh asked many questions. She found it hard to understand that there were no statues or idols of this unseen God. How can the Israelite people worship something they could not see? Even though Aweh was raised for a short time in a Hebrew camp when she was taken into slavery, she was neither an Israelite nor Hebrew, but knew of their worship of the unseen and unknown God.

Sheera explained that their village seldom had any diseases and when Aweh questioned why not, she told her how the Prophet Elisha would pass through their village and those who were very sick would become well. All who had faith were healed.

"Is your Prophet a magician?" Aweh asked. "No," she replied, "he is a Prophet of the Almighty God, Yahweh, and has powers that God gives him for different purposes. I don't know how he does his miracles, but he does it. He also teaches us our religious history and makes sure we understand the will of Yahweh as our Holy Father. We have great feasts and offer sacrifices when he comes," she answered.

"I am quite sure he can cleanse Master Naaman of his skin disease. He's done it many times, plus healed broken bones and helping women who were barren to become fertile."

"Where is this man located?" Aweh asked.

"Why, in Samaria," Sheera answered, "where I am from. He has been known to raise the dead, even curing poisonous water and food. He never refuses to cure someone, but his miracles have a lot to do with faith. If Naaman would go to him in faith, I am sure he would become clean." Upon hearing this news, Aweh put her fist to her mouth and stood; Sheera did the same.

"You should not fear Mistress Tirah. I had a short conversation with the Master. He was startled as well when you moved the curtain because you resembled Leda so much. He thought you were a ghost. He loved Leda as much as the Mistress. In actuality, even though she was a servant as we all are, she was their child."

"The Master will not say anything to his wife about your meeting. If he said he would not tell, the Master will keep your meeting to himself. But I must tell the Mistress of what you have just informed me." She then dismissed Sheera to her duties.

Aweh quickly ran into Amram who was coming from the Master's rooms. "Amram, Amram, come with me," she shouted. Amram looked at her as she grabbed his arm. "Have you ever heard of a prophet by the name of Elisha? He lives somewhere in Samaria."

Amram stopped quickly and looked at her. "Yes, he is a holy man, a miracle worker from Yahweh. He dwells in Samaria. All Israelites know of Prophet Elisha, even if they have never met him. Why do you ask?"

Quickly Aweh explained what the maid, Sheera, had told her — how the holy man worked miracles of healing and how he has healed numerous times. "If the Master would go to see him, Sheera believes he could be cleared of his disease. What do you think?"

Amram nodded his head and answered, "I am quite sure he could do anything our God allows. I will approach the Master about this. Commander Naaman is not a believer, but it would be wonderful for him to be cleansed. I will speak with the Master now."

15

Less than two weeks later, Sheera was summoned by Mistress Tirah. She sat before the Mistress and for the first time they talked of many things. When she asked about Sheera's family, Sheera explained how her village was raided by the soldiers and how she came to be on the slave block to be sold.

"I prayed you would choose me and Yahweh answered my prayers," she explained as she smiled at the Mistress. "The only thing I really miss from home is my family."

She went on to describe her father and brothers, how she was a well-loved daughter and sister. Her main regret was not knowing what happened to her family following the raid, as well as the young girl who was captive with her named Risa. Mistress asked her the names of her family and said she would talk to some of her husband's soldiers to see what information she could glean.

The Mistress stood and walked to the side of the room and kept her back to the young girl. Sheera stood to leave thinking the audience had ended, but Mistress Tirah turned and halted her and asked about the healing

Prophet who lived in Samaria. Aweh had told her the details of their conversation a few weeks ago and about the Prophet who could heal.

Sheera sat back down and began to explain what she knew of the Prophet Elisha and his healing powers. She explained how the Prophet spoke to the unseen God, Yahweh, and how Yahweh spoke to him in return. Mistress Tirah's questions were similar to what Aweh had asked before. No, he was not a magician or a psychic, but he was a holy man. His healing powers came from God.

The Commander had silently entered the room and stood still to listen to their conversation. He still had his face and arms covered. His valet, Amram, had just left him and explained that the Prophet was a healer of any and all diseases. The maid's explanation was similar to Amram's.

When Tirah saw her husband, she held out her hand as he took it and came toward her. To be cleansed of the disease was not just his heart's desire; he also wanted it for his wife. Naaman loved her and desired that she would be able to live a full life. Was this Prophet only another healer who would be paid for not doing anything? What if he decided to go all the way to Samaria and nothing happened?

He had been seen by so many Syrian healers and even a few magicians in Rimmon's temple and still the disease was spreading. He did not know when he would start losing body parts, perhaps first his nose or one of his ears. In his travels, he had observed lepers and had seen the progression of the disease. It was horrible. His skin had already begun to have burning sensations and knew that soon he would have no feeling in his limbs.

A short discussion of this unknown and unseen God was explained by the maid and the fact that the Israelites were chosen by God to be His special people. If the Israelites were so special, why were they now slaves in Syria?

Sheera continued. "I believe if the Master would go to see the Prophet Elisha who lives in Samaria, I know he would clear him of any medical problems. He's healed others who are not Samaritan." Sheera did not want to go into too much detail about the Master's leprosy and how much she knew about his ailment.

After a while, Mistress Tirah ceased asking questions; she gave her a warm smile as she patted her hand, and sent her back to her duties in the spinning room. The Commander and his wife watched as the maid left the room. They then sat back down and began discussing what they had just heard.

16

It was so dark in the last tunnel that he could hardly see his hands in front of his face. Elah's only consolation was the fact that Obid was near him. After the long trek through forest and desert, they were sent here to work in the mines. Twice he'd been whipped for trying to keep his son out of harm's way. Obid was so hot-headed Elah was afraid that Obid's beatings would be more than five or ten lashes. Little did he know that Obid had also been looking to his father's welfare. When Elah would have been beaten or lashed, Obid had tried to take his punishments.

The raid on his village was nothing but a slaughter. Many of the older men died relentlessly and the more the men fought, the worse the slaughter. He saw a few of his friends die, but knew they would rather die fighting than not. Obid had gone to fight a man on a horse to save a few of the women and girls who had been picked up by the raiders. He and his son fought on the women's behalf before the blunt end of another soldier's sword handle brought him down.

When he regained consciousness, he did not know if the women survived or were killed. His entire village was quickly being set on fire and he could see bodies lying around many of the burnt homes. The captured men that were still alive were put into an animal corral and guarded by many raiders.

Animals were killed and placed on boards and fresh fruit and vegetables were packed up by the raiders. The smell of blood, sweat and smoke permeated throughout the burning village.

On the other side of the village he saw Sheera's lifeless body lying across the pommel of a soldier's huge horse and there was no sign of Amir. What would become of his daughter? He began praying that she would not be raped or tortured by the raiders. "Please Yahweh, please do not let Sheera be used by these people," he pleaded. Was Amir dead? Would they kill a little boy? How ruthless were these men?

The soldiers began picking up men who were still alive, mostly young strong men, and tying their legs to each other, using their spears to egg them forward. The raiders rode their horses while the captured men were made to walk to an unknown destination.

It did not take Elah or Obid long to realize the raiders were not regular soldiers in the Syrian army. They were outlaws who thrived on getting captive slaves to sell for work in the Syrian mines. Not all the men had uniforms and some did not speak the same language. The Syrian language was Aramaic. Elah did not know the language, but he could make out some of the words. He noticed a lot of hand signals were given to each other in order to make themselves understood. Most had been together so long each knew without being told what was expected of them in the raid.

The captives had walked and walked for many days before they reached the outskirts of a large city, which was later identified as Damascus. A few of the men who were badly injured died along the way. The raiders would untie their ankles, drop the dead men in the dirt or sand, and retie the ankles of the other walkers, leaving the dead men's bodies to rot in the desert.

17

Some of the men were taken to the slave block and others were sent directly to the mines. By watching the raiders and their hand signals, both Elah and Obid realized Elah would have been taken to the slave block, but Obid held tightly to his father's arm when the decisions were being made by the raiders. When they began separating the men, Obid pulled his father toward him and both were sent to the mines.

A few years later, Obid told his father he always wondered if it would have been better for his father to be a slave rather than work in the mines. Elah understood his son's reasoning. He had been badly beaten during the raid trying to get to his daughter and baby son. For a while, he wondered why he was not killed. When the raiders saw he was a strong fighter, they laughed at his attempts and beat him instead. "This one will be a good worker," they laughed. "He's a fighter that one!"

For the majority of the walk following the raid, Elah stumbled along. When the captives were stopped to rest, in his weakened state Elah slept heavily, only to be awakened by a Syrian kicking at him to get up. Obid knew they would either kill his father or leave him to die in the desert so he constantly held him up.

When they reached the outskirts of the big city, there was no time to rest. The captives were quickly taken directly to the mines and worked throughout the day. They received a sickly-looking gruel to eat and murky water to drink. The work was grueling, the sleep was four to five hours and the food and water was little or nothing.

Mud was every where and sometimes the mud came to their knees. If a man fell, the other workers would quickly pick him back up. It was known that if the mud got into a man's nose and mouth, he would become asphyxiated. Sometimes a miner's body was not found for a few days as the digging moved on and when finally found, the rats, snakes and insects would have feasted on the body. The men rarely saw sunlight for they went to the mines in the dark of morning and back to their make-shift sleep tents in late evening or dark of night.

However, one day new Tyrrhenian and Sidonian captives were brought in and with them came freshly-killed animals that had been roasted. Just like at his village, the raiders brought in the fresh meat and vegetables that had been stored in the new captives' villages. Their spoils were too great for the raiders to eat before spoilage, so the animals were roasted and sold to the slave handlers, who, in turn, took the good meat and fed the rest to the slaves.

All the men fell upon the meat and fresh vegetables as it was brought to them. But that was only one day. That nourishment was the first good meal the miners were allowed to eat.

Less than 10-15 days later, more of the same meat was brought to the miners, but many believed the meat to be rancid and the majority of the slaves would not eat it. Some were so hungry they ate the meat, became ill from food poisoning and were whipped for being "lazy". The others knew if they ate the smelly meat, they would become ill and an ill miner could not work.

None wanted the lash of the whip for being unable to work for the overseers did not show leniency for illness. You were a slave and slaves were there to work.

Obid stayed his father's hand when he had reached for the spoiled meat, for which Elah was grateful after seeing other captives vomiting and then being whipped for being unable to work.

Over time Elah's strength returned and he and Obid worked side by side. When Elah's daily amount of ore was not attained, Obid put some of his ore with Elah's. When the overseer realized they were father and son, the two were separated from working side by side.

Their make-shift axes were not the best for mining, but Obid made new axes out of his and his father's axes and picks, making their digging a bit easier. Obid showed some of the other slaves how to make their tools more workable and they appreciated the young man. Even when Shobach, the slave master saw that the tools looked different, he said nothing since it seemed the men were able to work more steadily with them. As long as the men worked, he didn't care how their tools looked.

18

It was mid-afternoon when the first rumblings began. For Elah, it brought to mind the rumblings of the raiders' horses when they descended upon his village. His heart tightened in his chest as he froze for a few seconds, then he and others began running quickly toward the front. The mud was thick around their ankles, slowing their progress.

Cave-ins had been occurring too often lately and the sound became deafening as the cave's ceiling began spitting large rocks on the men, then boulders and wood beams began falling. There was yelling and screaming as the rocks were being thrown around them. The men who were not fast enough were caught in the earthly downpour.

Father and son had been separated but were still in the same tunnel when the cave's ceiling dropped large rocks. Obid was on the other side of the far section and felt the rumblings under his foot. It did not take the men on his side very long to realize the cave was beginning to collapse in front of them. The miners began running toward the entrance, which was far away.

Elah screamed his son's name, but the tunnel closed behind him and he was knocked toward the cave's wall. The last thing he heard when the ceiling fell in was Obid's far away voice crying for him. Quickly afterwards before he knew it, rocks and wood were laying across his legs. He could see a few bodies under the many rocks, for some of his co-workers were face down in the thick dark mud. He knew without checking that one of his legs was broken as well as a few of his ribs; and he also knew that he was an expendable slave. No rescue would take place for the buried slaves. He knew another captured slave would replace him once he died.

Practically giving up, Elah began to pray that Yahweh would be merciful and death would be swift. He began to see visions of his dead wife and his parents standing beside him and it wasn't long before he blacked out from the pain.

Elah slowly awakened and realized he was being bounced around on a wooden plank with a man at his foot and one at his head. The young man at his head was a bit older than Obid, but he had a smile on his face.

"Ah, I see you are awake," said the one at his head. "When I realized you were breathing I called other men over to help place you on this wood. Don't try to talk or move. Your leg is broken and I've put it in a make-shift splint for now. You also have a cut on your head that requires care. We'll take care of that later. Now close your eyes and go back to sleep. I have given you a draught for your pain which should make you sleep." Elah did as he was told and even though he was still in pain, he immediately fell back to sleep.

19

"Father, Father!" cried Obid as the cave crumbled in front of him. He watched some of the miners fall with the rocks and boulders from the cave's ceiling and knew they were crushed. It was only a few minutes, but seemed like hours before the noise stopped. Among the dust that was settling, he tried moving some of the huge rocks, but an older miner pulled him back. "No one could live through that," he said. "Come, there is another exit this way. We don't want to stay here for we don't know if more of the ceiling will come down upon us."

Those on the same side as Obid followed the older man about 100 meters and eventually saw a bit of moonlight, which let them know they had reached the other opening.

"My sister, my brother, and now my father," Obid mourned as he came out into the evening light. His eyes hurt from the light, but noticed the other men with him were also saddened. How many of them lost someone during this cave-in? How many of them lost family members and friends in other cave-ins? Did the Syrians have no mercy for the dead or the bereaved relatives?

For the next five days, the slaves in his group did not work on digging ore. They were sent to remove the huge rocks from the caved-in section for there was valuable ore in that area. Crushed bodies were found, silently mourned, removed and sent to a section on the outskirts of the mountain to be burned. When the cleanup was completed, the miners were again sent into the same section to continue digging for ore.

Each time a body was found, Obid would hurry over and check their faces and even though he was happy to not find his father, he mourned the dead men. In the dark, everyone looked the same and he began to wonder if Elah may have been found by other miners and burned without his knowledge. The only thing he could do was pray that his father's death was not a lingering one.

It did not take long for the raiders to arrive in the city and head for the slave block and the mines. Once again new captives were brought to the mines. Shobach, along with the guards and the overseer, brought the men into the caves to replace the dead. No one stopped to see who they might be. Whether men were from one's own village, no one knew. The men were separated into groups and sent with guards to the many areas in the hills to work silver and gold ore for the Syrians.

Obid watched as two new captives tried to fight one of the overseers, but the guards immediately took their clubs and beat them senseless. The whips came out and the slaves' backs were split open by the many lashes. One could see that the guards got great pleasure in beating and whipping them. When the beatings were finished, many of the slaves in the mines were called to drag their broken, bloody, and slashed bodies to the rear of the mine areas. Obid knew they were either to be killed if still alive, or burned if already dead.

The next morning, his father was replaced by a young Israelite by the name of Ewslet, and the slave master, Shobach, placed him in his group. Ewslet was not from his village, but it was good to be able to converse with someone in his own language.

20

In early afternoon, during the mid-day meal, there was a loud noise and then shouting was heard. Slaves and servants began running toward the mountainous area. People had stopped to see what was happening. Many soldiers also ran and as Aweh looked out of the main doorway she caught one of the servants. "What is happening?" she questioned. "There has been another cave-in at the mines," one shouted back.

Aweh hated hearing that one of the mines has caved in. Lives were lost and others were generally so badly hurt that many had to be put out of their misery. If the slave was hurt or lost a leg or an arm, when he was well enough the man was still forced to go back into the mines. She had traveled near there with one of the soldiers and knew of the misery the slaves suffered. But the Syrians always made sure there were many slaves to work in the caves to mine the silver and gold. She also knew the raiders would attack more villages and bring back new slaves. The raiders always received gold as payment for healthy slaves. There were always enough captives to work the mines.

It was one of the things she hated. Her own father and brother had worked in the mines and lost their lives through a devastating cave-in when she was little. When her mother found out her husband and son had died, she refused to live any longer. Aweh barely remembered her father and brother, and her mother was always ill following the cave-in prior to her death. She believed her mother died of a broken heart.

Aweh was very young when her family died. That was when she was sold with a group of slaves to the Commander's father and went to live with other slaves in his compound. When the old Commander was killed in battle and his son, Naaman, rose up the ranks, Aweh was brought to the Hebrew slave quarters and was later raised by an older woman from Psidia. She had a pretty normal upbringing under the Commander, but it was shown early that her aptitude for learning was very high for a few of the educated slaves taught her many things.

She had learned to speak many languages and was in charge of communicating with the other slaves in their native tongues. When an argument ensued, the other slaves would ask her to arbitrate arguments and interpret the languages of the new slaves. She was able to make sure accurate instructions were given that the new slave could understand.

Aweh was quickly noticed by the new Mistress for her linguistic abilities and was brought to the Master's quarters to be a servant for his wife. She later became more than a servant to the Mistress, she soon became her teacher.

Since the Commander's illness, Tirah was very lonely so Aweh began teaching Mistress Tirah the Hebrew and Sidonian languages. The Commander believed it would allow his wife to have something to do. The Mistress was an apt learner and enjoyed having lessons with the young slave girl. Over time, they became great friends and since there were many men around for the Commander but few women for the Mistress, it was good for her to have someone to confide in. Eventually, Aweh made sure the Mistress was kept up to date with what was going on in the compound.

Aweh went to her quarters to light many candles and prayed to her small icons and statues for the safe journey of the dead men's souls.

21

Over six or seven weeks passed and Sheera noticed that the Mistress had not been visiting the curtained room for some time. This generally let her know that the Master was not in the city. He had never been away for such a long period unless there was a war and she had no idea if this was something that happened often so she did not question anyone about it.

Later, while walking beside the carrier in the heart of the city, Sheera saw the back of a small boy carrying a sack of meal walking behind six other young boys who were also carrying small sacks. The boys were between the ages of five and ten or eleven and walked in a straight line.

The larger boys carried two sacks and the smaller boys one. She had seen this young boy a few times before but only from the back of his head. It could be Amir, she thought. The only difference was this boy was a bit taller and more muscular. Of course, as some time had passed, she knew that her brother would be much taller since the raid.

As she craned her neck to see better, she walked into the maid in front of her, almost tripping them both. "So sorry, so sorry," she apologized. Mistress Tirah poked her head out of the curtained carrier and questioned what was happening. "I'm sorry, Mistress. I was walking too fast and walked into Pua."

"Be careful," the Mistress admonished. "One wrong step and you will trip the men."

"What's the matter with you, Sheera?" Pua whispered. "You've been acting weird for the last couple of months. Are you ill?" Sheera turned around to look for the young boy, but he had already disappeared into the crowd. "There is a young boy who looks a lot like my younger brother, Amir, in the crowd. I've seen him before and in trying to see his face, I tripped into you. Please forgive me. It's probably not him." Pua shrugged her shoulders and continued walking forward beside the carrier. "Do not get your hopes up too high," she cautioned. "That way your hopes will not be dashed to the ground."

For days Sheera had thought of the boy. Could it be that Amir was alive? And if so, what of Obid and her father? Were they all slaves and not killed? She realized that her sighting of this boy could be an answer from Yahweh, for her prayers were to find out if any of her family still lived.

Mistress Tirah had not gotten back to her about her request for information. She only had this one hope.

22

Early one morning, Aweh stood in the door to the Mistress' quarters and smiled at her as she led one of the Master's personal servants toward her. Mistress Tirah looked up and saw the flushed face of a man who was breathing very hard. Her husband's personal servant – good news or bad?

"Has something happened, Dahameen? Is my husband in good health?" The Mistress had turned ghostly pale.

"Oh, no, Mistress Tirah; I mean yes, he's in good health," he breathed heavily and leaned against the beams of the room. "He is quite fine. He will be here in a few days' time. He sent me ahead to inform you that all is well. All is very, very well. I ran because I wanted to get here as quickly as possible. I was instructed by him not to say little more than that, for the Master has great news. When I catch my breath, I will tell you more. I am to only tell you what he told me to tell you in your hearing only."

"Aweh, take Dahameen to the outer room. Make sure he has food, wine and a place to rest." Mistress Tirah instructed. "Then, Dahameen, come to me as soon as you have rested, but do not wait too long. I must know the news." The Mistress turned, went to the nearest stool and sat. She did not know what to expect, but she could see that Dahameen was excited. It must be good news.

Two hours later, Dahameen and the Mistress talked in the small section of the house that would have housed her children, had she been able to bear them. She now used it as a room for comfort where she could cry without being seen or heard by the servants.

As Dahameen excitedly related the news the Master told him to repeat, she began to cry. Dahameen stopped several times as he told her of the trip to Samaria and how the entourage met with King Jehoram. He did not want to give out too much information for it was his Master's right to tell his wife the entire story.

Mistress Tirah noticed he was holding back some information whenever he would hesitate in the telling. Finally, he said, "Your husband is on his way home and will be here in a few days or so, or perhaps within two days if he does not stop too often to rest the animals, my lady. I can tell you no more, but you will be immensely happy."

Dahameen bowed low before her and, as he prepared to take his leave, gave her the biggest smile she had ever seen on him in all the years he has been a servant for the Commander.

As he passed her to head for the doorway, she could see he wanted to pat her shoulder, but out of respect did not do so. On impulse, she grabbed his hand and said,

"Thank you, Dahameen. You are a wonderful man. Go home now to your family and when you hear my husband has returned, you may return to attend him."

Dahameen was an Israelite who came as a small child from a raid under the Commander's father. Her husband, like his father, trusted him explicitly and always took him with his soldiers to attend him.

When Naaman was wounded in battle, it was Dahameen and the Commander's valet, Amram, who used Israelite poultices to help heal him and hid him in a cave until he was able to be moved. If the Master had awaited care by returning home, he would surely have died. Even the Syrian soldiers had great respect for him, unlike the attitudes they generally showed toward slaves and servants.

Dahameen had married one of the pretty servant girls from the spinning room and they had three small children. The Master had given him a small house near the compound so that he would not be far from attending him. Of all her husband's attendants, she loved and trusted Dahameen and his brother, Amram, the most. She knew this was why her husband entrusted him to bring the news.

23

The next day, as Sheera was working in the spinning room, spinning and making cloth for pants for the Mistress' bearers, she was once again called by Aweh to an audience with Mistress Tirah. Aweh seemed to be very excited and Sheera could see that she was exceedingly happy.

"The Mistress desires an audience with you," she said as she clapped her hands together. There was a glow about her that Aweh only exhibited when the Commander returned from his rounds, but this time there was a certain something that had never been there before.

"What is it? I don't think I've done anything wrong. Oh, no, the Mistress has not complained about my work, has she?" she asked. "No, no," Aweh said. "There is good news. I will let the Mistress tell you."

Sheera changed from her working robe to the soft green one she had made for herself in the spinning room. There was extra pale green material left from various curtains that were made for some of the areas around the house. There was always material left over, so she retained all the larger pieces and in her spare time would go to the spinning room, finish her duties, and sew. For herself, she would sometimes sit and embroider small flowers or animals on the hemlines. This robe hung gracefully on her body. She knew the discarded material left enough for her to begin sewing extra servant robes for the women who served in the compound.

Pua, as well as Shatii, loved their new outfits. They exclaimed that when they did their work outside of the compound, other servants would comment on their new clothing. Sheera had even made Aweh a special dress and would soon present it to her to wear on a special occasion when she went out with the Mistress. She knew Aweh would look very nice in the new robe she had sewed. It was finer than her own for she was aware that Aweh, being a senior and more important maid, would appreciate it.

She also believed Mistress Tirah was purchasing extra material instead of the actual amount needed for her rooms so other clothing could be sewed for her house servants. Some of the other women in the compound began dressing in their new robes for the compounds' special occasions. The slaves didn't have many occasions, so any time they could, they donned their new robes.

She could tell her body was becoming more formed and noticed how the male servants would look after her even in her tan robes as she walked around the compound. She had also grown an inch or so and felt very mature since her body had rounded. With the good food and care, her hair glistened in the sun and her skin had a golden glow, not like the ruddiness from being in the sun all the time as when she lived in the village.

New sandals had been provided for her since her feet were now another size and she was able to walk quietly inside the house. In fact, she did not look like a lowly servant in her new robe, but as a lady's maid. Knowing her true position, however, she did not normally dress in her new robes within the compound, but when Mistress Tirah traveled in her carrier, she would request that Sheera, Pua, and Shatii and the new fourth maid, Leatha, wear their new robes as they walked beside it.

24

The Master had been away for over two months, but before he left, the Master and Mistress had talked long into the night. Sheera had not heard of any wars he and his men might be fighting, but since he left, the Mistress had been very quiet, only speaking to her when necessary. It was now strange that she was being summoned in the middle of the day.

She quickly headed down the second hallway to Mistress Tirah's eating area with trepidation and a small amount of fear. Aweh met her in the middle of the hallway which would lead her to Mistress Tirah.

"Is it about my family? Has the Mistress discovered anything?" Aweh looked away. "It is not news about you, but about the Mistress and the Master!" She looked almost apologetic as she said, "I am sorry, Sheera, I do not believe we have heard any news about your family, but I think you will still be pleased."

Fear again crept in. One of the female maids, Aleea, who arrived in the compound with her from the slave block had been sold to one of the Mistress' friends. That was the same answer Aleea was told, that she "will be pleased" with her new assignment. Was she to be sold also? She did not want to be removed from this house.

Servants really had no options for they were nothing but property. She enjoyed serving the Mistress, and working in the kitchen and spinning room. Sheera was not stupid and knew changes happened among the servants all the time. There had been servants who were sold or traded, beaten or removed from the area; and there were others who ran away. Those who ran away and were caught she did not want to think about.

Always in her mind was the picture of the young girl who tried to run away during the trek toward Damascus. She could still see the spear that came out of her chest. Before the memory would show up in her dreams, but over the last few years, she was able to put it behind her.

Throughout the entire time she lived here, she'd only seen one male slave beaten and dragged out by the soldiers. It was when she first arrived in the compound. The other slaves helped to capture him, but everything she was told was hearsay. Some of the older servants related that he was sent to work in one of the silver or gold mines, but she also knew that he might have later been put to death.

It was for a good reason, for the slave had tried to grab one of the young female slaves during late evening. It was reported that he had tried to do so once before, but she always traveled with the other slave girls. This time, however, she was alone and when she screamed, the other male servants ran and grabbed him and began to punch and kick him. In reality, the soldiers saved his life, for the girl was the younger sister of another male servant. If the perpetrator had been in her village, he would have been stoned right away and his body left for the insects and birds.

As they moved down the hallway with arched openings, Sheera again noticed the young boy who looked similar to Amir walking with other boys, following behind a flat carriage with six bearers. From the bands on their arms, the young boys were not a part of the carrier group ahead.

One of the bearers of the carrier was a muscular young man who looked very familiar. She smiled at the bearer as she hesitated to get a better look for the boy, but once again, the boy disappeared. The bearer turned toward her and smiled as he gave her a quick wink. Stunned, she quickly backed away from the opening and aligned her pace with Aweh's so it would not be noticed that she had hesitated. This was the same young man who had winked at her when she had been newly purchased by the Mistress.

Sheera entered the room as Aweh turned and left. Mistress Tirah was wearing a wide smile; then, motioning with her hands, she requested Sheera to sit in front of the low table. Once again, the same older woman came in with various dishes on a tray and sat the tray down on the table. She looked into Sheera's eyes and gave a friendly grin, which Sheera automatically returned.

The woman situated the bowls and plates around in the middle of the table and bent to bow before the Mistress before leaving. She then put a few plain bowls in front of Sheera and on her way to the door, she patted Sheera on the back.

While the Mistress had her back to them, the older woman bent and put her head close to Sheera's ear and whispered, "I have news for you." Silently she left the room.

Mistress Tirah noticed Sheera's smile and said, "Her name is Sunih and she has been with my husband a long time, even before I married him. A wise woman who keeps me apprised of everything that goes on in the compound for I seldom go out, except of course, to visit my friends, shop, or do a few personal errands. I notice she likes you. Sunih serves me and she is totally loyal to me and my husband. She basically runs this household, especially the spinning room and the kitchen area, and also oversees the cooking of my meals. She could have any of the servants serve me, but she chooses to do that herself."

Mistress Tirah gave a wide smile and Sheera saw for the first time that her smile reached her eyes. Tirah asked about her duties and complimented her on the new dishes she had taught the servants in the kitchen to prepare. "They are similar to dishes we ate back home," Sheera explained. "It's rough fare, but has meat and vegetables that I know you like. The herb garden in the rear of the compound has herbs that enhance the flavor. The food is filling and I'm pleased you enjoy it." They both smiled at each other.

The Mistress commented on Sheera's new robe and how well she sewed. "The women in the spinning room are very pleased with the new robes you've made for them. As a matter of fact, they no longer look like servants. With the new clothes, they are fixing their hair and have made new sandals for themselves and now walk so sedate. My friends tell me that my servants look much better than theirs and are now thinking of outfitting them with new robes and outerwear. Thank you, Sheera; our household has started a new fashion trend." She continued to smile and shifted her body to become more comfortable.

"By the way Sheera, your friend, Aleea, who worked with you, now serves one of my friends, Mistress Petra. My friend's husband is General Meruru, who is under my husband. Aleea is a good worker and my friend finds her enjoyable. At first I did not want to give her up, but my friend's maid has married and she is now pregnant. Petra asked if I would allow Aleea to come work with her as her new maid and my husband and I were agreeable. She will be well treated and her duties are now similar to yours. A message from my friend informs me that Aleea is very happy there and sends you, Pua and the others her greetings."

Sheera was pleased. She and Pua thought Aleea had been sold. Pua and Shatii were all purchased by the Mistress at the same time and worked closely with Aleea. When she returned to her quarters, she would tell Pua and Shatii the news. No selling was involved in the move. She knew this would also set their minds to rest about their friend.

"What I want to tell you is that my husband is on his way home. And thanks to you, we will be able to be close again." Sheera looked questioningly at her. "My husband took some of his trusted soldiers and servants to Samaria and met with your Israelite Prophet. The Prophet has healed him of the leprous disease he has been challenged with for years." The Mistress could hardly talk; she was so happy, she was almost babbling.

"All of our Syrian doctors could not do much for him, and they had no powers of healing for the disease. Of course, many doctors do not want to touch a man in my husband's condition, but would do so because of who he is – yet, still charging exorbitant amounts, only to tell him there was nothing they could do. I will let my husband tell you the entire details after he returns. Thank you so much for your help."

With that, Mistress Tirah did something she had never done in the entire years Sheera had lived in the compound. She stood up, causing Sheera to also stand, reached over and gave her a big hug. Sheera was stunned and could do no more than hug her in return and hesitantly pat her back.

"One of his servants was sent ahead to tell me what happened on the trip, that my husband is on his way home and will soon return in one or two days' time. The servant was very happy and cried with me while relating portions of the events of the trip to me -- and now I, too, am elated. Tomorrow you and I will remove the curtains of the back room and my husband's servants will have them burned; then you will be able to scrub everything there. Afterwards, you, Pua and Shatii will follow the men to go clean another part of the house, for my husband and I will soon be able to resume our marriage quarters."

Sheera stammered her happiness for the Mistress as she dismissed Sheera to search out Aweh.

She had been in Syria for a long time and had never seen Mistress Tirah so happy. She would soon be reunited with her husband. Sheera gave a quick sigh as she also wished to be reunited with her loved ones. She was quite sure her family was dead, but not so sure about Amir. Even though some years had passed, she was now quite sure the boy she saw was her baby brother Amir.

25

Commander Naaman had just arrived at the stables of the compound. He could not wait to see his wife. Tirah would be so happy, just as he was happy. This must be what joy feels like. Dahameen and Amram always talked about the feeling of 'joy'. It was more than being happy, but more like a happiness fulfilled. Naaman had to stop himself from skipping like a young boy toward the front of the house. After handing his horse to one of his grooms, he continued on.

He and Amram headed toward the bathing area to wash the travel stains away as Dahameen came forward with three male slaves. Dahameen had the slaves take the donkeys and horses to the rear of the stables. He showed them an area to the side of the compound for the storage of the soil from Samaria. He knew the Commander would later tell him where he wanted the soil placed.

Amram could see the Commander was antsy, so he quickly bathed him and handed Naaman a light robe for it was a warm evening. He and Amram talked quietly as they headed toward the curtained area. He saw that the curtains were gone and the area had been cleaned.

Mistress Tirah met the two men and nodded toward the sleeping area that had not been occupied by them for years. Inside were a great bed, a small couch and other furniture, as well as a lit silver candle holder in the corner. The room smelled of perfume and lilac. Sheera had placed a vase with small desert flowers on a table on the side of the room.

The Commander then released Amram from his duties. He smiled at his wife and entered the room. As he headed toward her, she could see his handsome face clearly in the candlelight.

Naaman came into the dimly lit outside section of the bedroom in his robe. Tirah was sitting on the edge of a small couch and he sat down beside her, took her hands in his, and began his story.

* * *

"As you know, I left to travel to Samaria almost two months ago. You are an intelligent and good wife, Tirah. You told me to take my most loyal servants and soldiers with me and I did — I hand-picked them myself. My King wrote a letter to the king of Israel to allow me passage through Samaria and to find the Israelite Prophet your maid talked about.

I realize I am a proud man and my pride almost stopped me from doing what needed to be done to help me with this affliction." Naaman stopped to consider what he had just said to his wife.

"The Israelite king, Jehoram, is not a man of business. When we arrived, King Jehoram thought we had intents of starting a war and was very suspicious of us. There were only 25 of us, my Legion soldiers and a few servants, yet he felt there was another intent. Of course, I arrived looking very prosperous and brought with me horses and chariots, which probably caused the fear.

I realized his character when I handed him the note from King Ben-Hadad. If he had read the note fully, he would have known that I came for healing by the Prophet, but he let me know that he could not heal me. I told him it was not him I wanted to see, but the great Prophet Elisha, as your maid had said.

Then I thought to myself, what if your maid was wrong? What if he is unable to heal me and we have come on this long journey for naught? What if he only heals Israelites? I know very little about the Israelite's God and their prophets. What I do know I learned from Amram, Dahameen and other servants. I had a bunch of 'what ifs'."

"I found out later from my servants that the Prophet had heard I was looking for him even before I presented the letter to the King. His God must have talked with him about me. When the Israelite king was so suspicious, my servants told me that the Prophet Elisha had already sent a messenger so I would have directions to his dwelling. The messenger said the Prophet told my servants that he wanted to let Naaman know there was a true man of God in Israel. His directions were accurate and I had no problem finding him."

"We were given explicit directions to this Prophet's dwelling and yet, when we arrived, he did not even come out to meet me."

"I, a great commander in the Syrian army! I was disgusted! We traveled all the way from Aram with men, gold, silver and other gifts, made a visit to that ignorant Israelite king and then, when we got to the Prophet's dwelling, he sends out a little man to meet me -- a servant named 'Gehazi'. Gehazi – what type of name is that? Did you know that in Hebrew his name means 'vision?' Who would name their child Vision?"

Mistress Tirah gave a quick giggle and said, "The Israelite ways are not like ours. Their names have meanings that none of us fully understand. But, to their credit, we have names that they don't understand either. I wonder what Sheera's name really means? She is a pretty girl and full of wisdom. But do go on." She was anxious to hear the story of the entire trip and their servants' names meant nothing to her at that moment.

"Yes – and can you believe this? — when the Prophet's little manservant reached us, he said the Prophet instructed that I should go and wash — no, he said dip — myself seven times in that nasty Jordan River and I would be healed. Seven times! Put my body in that horrible river and dip myself seven times? We have the Abana and Pharpar, as well as the rivers of Damascus. By the gods! I could have bathed in any of them and saved myself that long journey. Or so I thought. Anyway, I almost let pride stop me."

"I became angry with myself for following the tale of a servant girl. I began to think she may have just said that to get me out of the country in order to start a war — at that I became very, very angry. I told my men to prepare to turn around for we would return home to Damascus."

"As you know, a few of my servants are sons and nephews of our older Israelite slaves and their fathers told them what powers the Prophets of their unseen God have and what they have been known to do."

"Even my soldiers thought the instruction was strange, but they and the servants felt there must be something to it. They began discussing it among themselves and then argued with me. I felt they were being insubordinate, but they would not back down. Even Amram said we should do as we were told. After all, getting into the river to bathe — what harm would it do? Besides we were dusty from the travel. All I could think of was the silt and dirt known to be in the Jordan River."

"My servants and soldiers urged me and said surely it would not hurt me to wash in the River. After all, the Prophet could have told me run up a mountain naked, cut my body with a knife, or jump off the highest limb of a tree in the forest and I would have done it. How much more would it be to do such a simple act? Finally I gave in and they were right!"

"However, I had thought perhaps the Prophet Elisha would at least have come out of his house himself to tell me and say some type of incantation or even call on the name of his God, jump up and down, or wave his hands over my body or perhaps even touch my head and say a few prayers. But he didn't do any of that. He just gave some simple instructions by way of his little servant."

"After thinking over what my men said, I finally went ahead and followed the instructions. I thought to myself I would do anything to be free of this leprous condition and I'm already in this barbaric country."

"Yet, I had a most embarrassing moment when I had to remove my clothing and armor. Most of them, except for Amram and Dahameen, had never seen my body in its entirety with the peeling skin, boils and white spots that were from head to toe. I could see their surprise as the men tried not to stare at me, and I knew it was hard for them not to do so, for I was always covered in armor or a mask-like helmet."

"However, with their prodding, I eventually decided to go ahead with it. Azor, my armor bearer, and the servants took off my armor and clothing and they helped me get into the water for my washing. Being naked before them was something I never thought would happen. I could see the men's astonishment and pity. Amram suggested I go further into the water to make sure my entire body was covered. It was a very hard time for me."

"I even ordered a few of my men, as well as Amram, to get into the river with me to help me wash, but Amram told the men the Prophet told *me* to do it, not them. At first I thought it was because of the sight of my nakedness and my condition, but later found out they were following the orders of Amram, who told them not to listen to me, but to let me do as the Prophet instructed."

"Can you believe that? They all disobeyed me on the word of Amram, a servant!"

"After the first two dips, I was ready to stop and get out, for the water's silt and slime was around my shoulders, but my soldiers and servants egged me on. Eventually Amram and some of my men came into the water beside me, but would still not help me wash."

"Keep washing, they shouted and began counting with me as I dipped myself. And that Amram, my most trusted manservant, even pushed my head under the water to make sure my entire body was washed. At first I was angry with him, my soldiers, and myself, but soon the washing became a game to them."

"Azor even turned his back on me and held his sides as he laughed at my clumsiness. Soon they all began to laugh at my washing. Especially Amram – for, as you know, he is the one who always bathes me. But he was laughing so hard he was bent over, holding his sides too! He was unable to do anything, and his laughter became infectious and soon all of them were laughing. Eventually I, too, started laughing."

"The more I washed, the more I could feel my body changing. I could feel the boils and peeling skin slipping away from my arms and torso. Even my wounds from old battles were being healed without me realizing it. I did not know about that until much later. By the fifth washing, I knew something was truly happening. After the seventh time, I came up from the water and looked at myself and felt my face and hair."

"I, Commander Naaman, a grown man, friend of the king, and a leader of many soldiers — began to cry."

"Tirah my love, my face, hands, and body were as clean as that of a baby boy. I felt my head and my balding spots were now full of thick glossy hair. I began to sob; I cried, my soldiers cried, and my servants cried. We laughed and cried in front of each other — something none of us had ever done before. Not in victory or even when I was wounded in the war. Those men began doing a wild dance with each other like I'd never seen before." He stopped and laughed at the memory.

He coughed and then continued. "At this point, I was ready to remain in that river a lot longer and bathe seven more times, but they began pulling me toward shore. I had done what the Prophet told me and was rewarded for doing so." He completely stopped talking at this point and Tirah could see that he was holding back tears.

Naaman then reached over to the lamp stand, picked up a lit candle and bent to light the lantern closest to the couch. While smiling at her, Naaman stood up, moved into the lantern's light, opened his robe and let it drop to the floor. Stretching his arms and hands away from his body, he proceeded to face front showing his naked body to his wife.

Tirah began to cry. It had been many years since she had seen his body in full, for Naaman did not like her to see the boils and scaling that appeared as the disease progressed and ate its way across his face, hands, and body.

His body was magnificent! Stepping over his robe, he slowly turned and displayed his back as well.

She stood and went to him and they hugged and cried together for some time. He took her back to her seat, reached down to redress and tied together the ropes of his robe. Reseating her he said, "I have more to tell you."

"If it had not been for my soldiers and the servants, I would have returned to you the same as I left. I have not only been cleansed outside, but inside as well."

"Have I always been this pompous? Have I always been so stupid? My pride almost got in the way of my healing. I was not a believer in a God that I could not see and touch."

"When you told me what your maid, the Israelite servant girl said, I felt 'why not' since everything else I'd done had failed, but I was not very hopeful at that time. Even when I asked King Ben-Hadad for the letter of introduction to the Israelite king, I still had my doubts. I'm not an Israelite, but I now believe in this unseen God of the Israelites they call Yahweh."

"Our god, Rimmon, has done nothing for me. All the prayers and sacrifices we've offered to him have been to no avail. And yet this unseen God, whom I have never seen, worshipped or offered sacrifices, gave me my life. I want to find out more about Yahweh for He is, indeed, a great God."

"I wanted to thank the Prophet Elisha for what he had done for me," Naaman continued, "so my men and I left the river. We changed into dry clothing and headed back to the Prophet's house. This time he invited me into his house and I was then able to talk with him about my healing. He also told me about Yahweh and himself. And, Tirah, I was so happy that I brought back soil from Samaria." He began to laugh at himself.

"I just had to have something from the area near that river and since I couldn't scoop all that water, I decided it would be good to have the soil. I brought back two whole mule loads of it. I will only worship Yahweh from now on. And I am asking and hoping that you will worship this God along with me."

Tirah was still wiping her eyes, but she nodded her head yes.

"I did ask the Prophet if it would be all right if Yahweh would allow whenever my King and I go into the temple of Rimmon that I be excused because I no longer believe in our gods, but only in the One True God, Yahweh. The Prophet nodded a simple yes and told me to go in peace."

"And you know, I could not give the Prophet a thank you gift. I would gladly have given him anything, but he refused my gifts and said he did not need my gold, silver, or clothing – or anything. I did, however, have my servants give some things to his servant, Gehazi, who came after me to ask for gifts for other prophets. I was so overjoyed when he requested a talent of silver that I gave him two, as well as some of the garments I brought with me."

"After the first full day of being clean, while we rode toward home, I kept checking under my clothes to make sure the cleansing was not a temporary thing. My faith and my heart said I was fully cleansed, but my mind said the boils may reappear. They have not and I believe never will."

"I was also worried that any children we produced might inherit the disease, but I believe they will not. I have faith that Yahweh is a complete God as Dahameen and Amram have told me. We *will* produce healthy children, Tirah." He gave her the wonderful smile that she used to see years ago.

"I am still exuberant and wanted to let you know first hand what happened. When I sent word by Dahameen, I made him promise he would not stop to tell anyone but you. I have not yet shown myself to the King, which I will do on the morrow. We can now live as husband and wife and perhaps become fruitful."

"And to think, I almost did not receive my healing because of pride."

"I would like to later talk to your maid, Sheera, and our other Israelite servants about Yahweh. And I was wondering if there is anything I can do for Sheera for she was the one who was helpful to my healing."

He ran his fingers through his hair as he searched her face. "Would you mind if I gave Sheera her freedom to return to her Samaritan village? Would you miss her if I did so?"

Tirah smiled and answered, "Yes, I would mind and yes I would miss her. But there is a way you could be of service to her. During the raid on her village, she lost her father and brothers and does not know whether they are still alive. Her father is called Elah and her brothers are Obid and Amir. They were of a small village near the area called Aphek near Samaria. Obid should be a young man by now and Amir should be about the age of perhaps eleven or twelve. I am not sure if her father was killed, but is there any way you could find out?"

"Even if we freed her, it would be hard for her to go back there, for she says her village was plundered and set on fire. Also, there is another female slave that was sold about the same time I purchased Sheera by the name of Risa. She's probably Sheera's age or perhaps a bit younger." Naaman wrote the names down and said he would do his best.

"Had she been betrothed to a young man prior to her capture, do you know?" Naaman put his arms around her and pulled her close. "A few of my generals' men have seen her and would like to purchase her for marriage, but I informed them that she belongs to you and it would be your decision. She and your other maids are all of marriageable age. "

Tirah looked appalled. "Oh, no, I refuse to sell her or give her away! I was unhappy about letting Aleea go, but knew she would be safe and happy with Petra," cried the Mistress.

"Sheera once mentioned a young man who died in the raid who was her betrothed, but never told me his name. I believe she mentioned he was killed by the raiders who plundered her village. She has not discussed such things with me, but perhaps Aweh would know since she talks with all the servants. You are correct, she is now at an age for marriage, but she seems content at this point."

"Aweh, however, has her sights on someone, but I do not know who he is. I believe he may be one of your servants who travels with the loyal group in your regiment. She was very happy when Dahameen arrived the other day, possibly because she knew you would soon be coming with your entourage, including her special man. Could it be Azariah? He always stays around the compound as if he's waiting to see you. It may be Aweh he's waiting on. She is always happiest when your men return so it must be one of them."

I have not even talked with her about such things because she is invaluable to me. I sometimes forget Aweh is a slave, for she is like my younger sister."

"Come," said the Commander as he stood and took her hand. "We will discuss our servants later." Smiling, they both headed for the part of the house that had not been used in years.

26

A few months after the return of Master Naaman, while cleaning in the Mistress' old room, Sunih came to Sheera to pick up the eating utensils from the Master and Mistress' table. Sheera smiled at her and asked how her day was progressing. Sunih smiled and said, "As good as yours, little maid."

Sheera realized that Sunih had something to tell her so she stopped moving around the room and sat on one of the low stools when Sunih sat in another.

The older woman smiled and whispered, "Elah is well. He was working in the mines, but was injured when the mountain caved in. He was found by friends of my grandson and taken to one of General Meruru's servants' quarters. Master Naaman had recently asked his generals about your father and your brothers and General Meruru's overseer reported that he had an injured miner in the servant's quarters by the name of Elah."

"Elah is a common Israelite name, so the general did not think anything of it. My grandson works as a carrier bearer for General Meruru and his wife, and he was one of the men used to help carry the dead and wounded from the collapsed mine. He also has the gift of making medicine from herbs and poultices for healings."

"He was asked to take food to the slave quarters and met the men who were there recuperating. When he questioned one of the men as to where in Samaria he was captured, he realized the injured man could be the Elah the Commander was asking about. He reported this to General Meruru so that the General could report this back to Commander Naaman."

"I wanted to give you this good news – my grandson says that the man Elah is healing and is getting well. He said he resembles you and believes the man is your father."

Sheera cried out and rushed to Sunih's side and hugged her. "I am so happy," she sobbed. "I did not know. Thank you, thank you, thank you." As she clutched the older woman, Sunih said, "According to this Elah, your brother is in the mines also. My grandson has not seen him, but Elah told him this when he carried the men out of the mines. When they were first captured, they were working side by side, then the overseers split many relatives and they were separated. When part of the cave fell in, two men were killed. Your father was hurt on the shoulders and legs, but your brother had been sent to work in another part of the mine that day. He does not know where his son might be."

"Elah does not know whether his son is alive or dead. He was unable to see him when the cave-in happened, for he had been sent to another part of the mines." Sheera continued crying and nodded her head that she understood as she tried to smile through her tears.

"I have to go," the older woman stated as she stood, "but will talk to you again. My grandson was not able to talk to Elah for long, for he works for the General's wife and is on constant call."

Sunih picked up the used utensils and walked sedately out of the room as if nothing had taken place. I wonder if I should tell Commander Naaman this news also, she thought to herself.

A half hour later, Aweh came into the room and saw Sheera seated and crying. "Is anything wrong? Are you ill?" she asked. Sheera grabbed her by her arms and began babbling so much so that Aweh had a hard time understanding what she was saying. Slowly it dawned on her what Sheera was trying to tell her: The maid's father was alive!

27

Amir sat down to rub his arms. As he grew in age and size, he was now required to carry heavier packages for his Master. He was now almost eleven, yet he felt older. His mind went back to his village, his family, and the Syrian raid. He was grabbed by one of the soldiers and tossed onto the back of a huge stallion and was so afraid, it was all he could do to remain upright on the charging horse. The soldier had told him to be still or he would be tossed to the ground and the horse would probably kick him to death.

Some of the young boys his age were put on flat wagons while the older ones were told to walk – and they walked a long time for it was a few days before they reached the city of Damascus. The flat wagons bumped and tossed them about.

If anyone fell off, he was required to try to jump back on the wagons or run to keep up. Many times the other boys would offer their hands to the running child to make sure he was lifted back onto the wagons. A couple of the slower ones who were beaten or maimed during the fighting did not make it and were left in the desert to cry and die. No one would jump down and try to get them or they, too, would be left. Amir scooted against other small boys his size to make sure he remained in the middle of his wagon; he did not want to fall off.

After reaching the city late one evening, they were tied up and thrown into a large horse stall. The next day they taken to the slave block. Some of the older boys and men were sold or sent as slaves to the mines, but the soldier who captured him, named Ranah, kept him away from the slave block and immediately took him to his sister, Mahli.

Ranah's sister was around 13 or 14 years of age at that time, very thin, quiet, and immature. She was nice to him, but not as nice as his sister, Sheera. She seldom left her house and kept to herself. In his village, she would have been seen as an adult, but even though a teenager, she reminded him of a child younger than himself. She tended to throw tantrums to get her way, or want to play children's games with him, which he enjoyed. But sometimes she would sit in a corner rocking as she hummed to herself. The servants said she was "fey," which to him meant having a mental problem.

Amir missed Sheera so much, even after all these years. From a baby, she had acted as his mother, whom he had never met. The last time he saw her, she was running from another soldier.

Time meant nothing to him because it now seemed as if he had been in the city for more years than he could imagine. Within the first six months of being away from his family, he had matured and had begun to think of himself as a man. Slavery does that to you, he thought. The other boys he worked with also mourned their families and in the few years they had been together some had grown beards and mustaches and because of the heavy work, their muscles were those of athletes.

He knew Mahli had the power to have him beaten if he did not do as he was told. One of the older boys tried to run away and attempted to hide in a wagon to get out of the city, but when he was caught she had the boy beaten and sent to the mines.

He did not know where his father, Elah, or brother, Obid, had gone. They had been lined up with other adult male villagers and traveled a different route. The last he saw of Obid, his father was bleeding from trying to fight the soldiers, but he did not see his brother. Amir could only hope that his father and brother were not dead.

His slave quarters were not uncomfortable, and he was now used to his sleeping area. Even though the slaves were of different nations, they had learned to communicate with each other using hand signals and learning quite a bit of each other's native words. Mahli had thrown away some of her fur pieces and other materials and he had collected them and divided them among the other boys who used them to sleep upon.

Amir quickly learned the Aramaic language and was able to speak it fluently. He had remembered some sentences when the traders would pass through the village. Mahli did not know the Hebrew language very well, yet her brother was fluent in Hebrew, Sidonian and Chaldean, and possibly a few others.

In a few hours, he would go to Mahli and help her learn his language. Mahli was childlike, but was a quick learner considering her mental status, yet she was helpful in teaching him Aramaic. She did not attend school, so she tried to learn as much as she could from the slaves. Ranah did not believe his sister was capable of learning very much for at the age of five, Mahli's nurse dropped her by accident, and it was not long afterwards that he realized her learning progress was slow.

Amir wondered what happened to Mahli's nurse, and knowing she had been a slave believed the outcome would not have been good. It wasn't until she was almost 12 that he recognized she had some mental deficiencies – for even though Mahli grew in size, her mental capabilities did not. There were times when Mahli was almost Amir's playmate, and teaching lessons to her was similar to playing school games when he was younger, almost when Sheera was his teacher.

28

Amir had just returned from traveling with the kitchen servants to pick up grain and meat and it seemed the closer they came to Ranah's house, it was as if the bags were getting heavier and heavier. He used to carry one bag, but as he grew older and taller, he now carried two or three. After putting the bags on the table, his arms would shiver with relief from depositing their weight.

As a young slave, he was required to work with older and more seasoned slaves. And because of his youth, he was to also help carry packages, walk behind Mahli's carrier when they went to the city or the Syrian temple, and help in the kitchens. He sometimes worked the farmland that was owned by Ranah when one of the servants was ill or had died.

He enjoyed working the farmland, especially with the young lambs. The older sheep were serene and pretty much did what he wanted them to do. Of course, there was always a ram or ewe that was stubborn, but after he slapped them on their rear flanks a time or two, they would mind. There were slaves to shear the sheep as well as others who were the regular shepherds, but mainly his job was to keep the younger lambs in line.

He did not mind the other work, even though some jobs were tedious. The only job he really did not like was following Mahli and the other Syrians to worship their gods. While he was inside the temple of Rimmon, he would close his eyes and pray to Yahweh that his time there would pass quickly. Their religious ceremonies were noisy and loud with screaming, beating of drums, and grown men in red and white gowns dancing around a fire and bowing before a weird-looking statue, sometimes cutting themselves and screeching at the tops of their voices.

He was told that human sacrifices were sometimes made by the worshippers, but he had never been in attendance during that part of the ceremonies, for slaves were only allowed to enter Rimmon's temple just far enough to escort their Masters. He was told by the older slaves that if he ever chanced to view Rimmon's sacrifice altar, it would probably mean he was going to be the sacrifice for some slaves were used in those ceremonies.

He could only remember one word his father would use for such goings on and that was "pagan." He never understood that word until the first time he followed behind Ranah and Mahli into the temple. Afterwards, when he and the other boys returned to their quarters, they would silently offer prayers – each to his own god and he to Yahweh.

By going into the kitchens, he was able to learn more about Yahweh from the Israelite slaves for some still remembered the worship ceremonies held in their villages.

They secretly celebrated various feast days and ceremonies in accordance with the laws of Moses, continuing to follow their religion. Other slaves who worshipped the gods of their nation would also meet together to worship in their own way.

He laid down on his mat for awhile to rest but could not sleep. When it was time for him to go to Mahli's quarters, he washed the sleep from his eyes, flexed his muscles and started toward the house, entering by the side doors.

29

As he passed by the kitchens, Amir stopped and stared. A young girl had her head down and was washing the used pottery and cooking utensils. She looked up and stared back at him and recognizing Amir, she smiled.

Pridi! It's Pridi!!

Even though he knew Ari was dead, he never knew what happened to some of the females. Pridi was alive! He gave a wide smile in return, and then lifted his hand to give a quick wave in answer to her wave. Pridi was alive! Where had she been all these years? He should have seen her before if she had been working in the kitchens, for he made constant trips there to carry items for the cooks.

Strange, he had not given her a thought since he arrived in Damascus, for he was sure everyone from his village was dead. But he was exceedingly glad to know she was alive and near him. Happy now, he began to whistle softly as he walked toward Mahli's quarters. He would try to speak with her later.

He picked up his pace and entered the room Ranah had set aside for his sister as a small schoolroom. Her brother did not think she needed to learn another language, but it was clear that whatever Mahli wanted, Mahli received. Although a soldier, it was also clear that Ranah loved his younger sister very much. As Amir walked toward her, she tilted her head and asked, "Is something making you happy, or are you just glad to be here for my lessons?" He nodded his head and smiled, not really answering her question. He then sat on the floor cross-legged to begin their lessons.

Mahli taught him more words in Aramaic and then he interpreted what the word meant in Hebrew. Later, another slave would come to instruct Mahli with her numbers.

All the while, as he interpreted the words, he thought about Pridi working in the kitchens. She looked to be in good health and she wore the clothing and arm band of Ranah's household.

After that, he made a point of walking toward the kitchens, whether he was needed there or not. In the beginning, he and Pridi learned to communicate with their hands and eyes or shaking or nodding their heads, and eventually speaking to one another.

It was through Pridi that he learned her entire family was dead, some during the raid and others died from beatings; some of the men were sent to the mines or sold into slavery, but she also thought he and his family were killed. Pridi was very happy Amir was alive and that they worked within the same household.

30

A few days later, as he walked behind Mahli's carrier with the other young men, he struck up a conversation with the young slave in front of him. They discussed the city and the various clothing worn by other slaves. Amir mentioned that he noticed new slaves in the kitchen and his friend said there were two new girls there. He had also overheard some of the soldiers discussing the fact that they previously belonged to another soldier, but he was killed in battle. It seems the soldier's wife sold them to their Master because she no longer needed them.

He also informed Amir that Ranah purchased them for a song. Since the more slaves you owned showed your wealth, it was beneficial to Ranah to own more. Besides, if Ranah needed money, he could always sell them to someone else. Or if a slave did not act right, he would send him to the mines.

They had nothing to worry about for Ranah had received an inheritance as he was the first born and only son of his parents. He had a sister who was married to a soldier and they had two children, one a young boy who would inherit his wealth if he did not have children.

However, it was rumored among the slaves that Ranah had his eyes on a Syrian temple priestess who lived in the city, but had not yet introduced her to Mahli.

31

As they walked on, Amir noticed another carrier heading toward them from the market. On each side of the carrier, there were two young ladies (four altogether) following the muscled young men who held it. As he looked to his left, the curtains in the other carrier billowed aside and he could see a beautiful lady inside the carrier talking with a young girl who was walking on the opposite side. He could not see the girl's face, but her walk reminded him so much of Sheera that he tried to get a better glance.

Too late, the carrier continued on, but he noticed the slave entourage's clothing was not made of the coarse material as generally worn by other slaves. These slave women wore pale green robes and all looked happy, as if something was said to make them smile. Their arm bands were green, which denoted that this carrier belonged to a person of influence. The band on his arm was brown, and under it there was a brand.

Amir had been branded when he first arrived in the beginning, but Ranah was angry with his overseer for he said he did not mean for him to be branded because of his youth. He felt brands should only be put on the older slaves, not children.

After his skin had healed, Amir was given the brown band to wear. He was glad he had been branded earlier, because now that he was old enough to be branded he knew it would take longer to heal. Ranah's symbol was already on his arm. Unless he was sold, he would not need to be branded again. He had watched other slaves get branded and the screams of the slaves and the smell of burned skin was horrible.

32

"What kind of tale do you have to tell me," asked Shobach in Aramaic, "that would keep me from sending you back to the mines?" Obid stood stoically in front of the slave master and did not answer. He was breathing heavily, standing tall with his tied hands clenched behind him as he and another young man faced the slave master behind the table. Both of their fists were bruised and there was a cut over one eye of Obid's opponent, Ewslet.

The overseer stood in front and two guards had both men by their arms. "This slave is an angry worker and was fighting with this other slave. Neither will tell me who or what started the argument."

Shobach asked what language they spoke, and since neither answered, the overseer punched Obid in the back and growled, "They can speak our language when they feel like it."

The overseer looked almost gleeful at Obid and Ewslet, knowing both would be whipped for fighting as well as for being obstinate. He enjoyed watching the slaves fight, but really enjoyed watching them get whipped, for he was bloodthirsty to the point of drooling.

"What is your name and what is your nation?" Shobach continued to interrogate both young men. Ewslet looked at Obid and finally said in Aramaic, "We are both Samaritans, but from different villages. We were roughhousing, not fighting." Ewslet knew it was a lie, but he also knew they would both be punished no matter what he said. "We disagreed as to which village had the strongest men. I am Ewslet and he is Obid."

Still Obid said nothing.

"Obid, Obid," the slave master repeated tapping his whip against his thigh. "Now why is that name familiar? And you say you are Samaritans from Israel? There's something about that name I should remember."

"Guards!" he called, "place them both in the Hole until I figure out what it is that makes his name so familiar. You two can continue to fight while you're in the Hole – that is, if you can move around in that small space. Hahahaha!" One of the guards and the overseer, who was somewhat disappointed that he would not view a whipping, almost dragged them as they left the presence of Shobach.

33

Shobach was not an evil slave master, but since he worked with so many captive slaves, their plight meant nothing to him. He did not like to hear about fighting. It was a waste of too much energy that could be better used for mining the silver. The silver lode was not coming in as fast as usual due to the many cave-ins. It seemed the gold mines were faring much better. Fewer cave-ins, fewer fights,` and fewer deaths.

All slaves came from different nations, with odd ways, odd gods, and all were, he believed for the most part, very stupid. The Israelites only believed in one God and He was invisible. The others believed in gods that had ridiculous names, and many did not even try to learn the Syrian language. Luckily these two had been in Damascus long enough to learn Aramaic, or at least enough to communicate.

Later, during the evening meal, Shobach discussed his day with his wife. When he mentioned the fight in the mines, she laughed and said the slaves always had a grievance about something or other. Her husband answered through his chewing, "The one is called Ewslet and the other Obid. Yet, there is something about the name 'Obid' that bothers me."

As his wife cleared the eating area, she turned to him and remarked that it has been reported that Commander Naaman has been looking for a slave called Obid since he returned from Samaria.

"I have news about a slave called Obid, my husband. While drawing water at the well, the women generally discuss the day's news and our newest item is the fact that the Legionnaires have been questioning if anyone knows of a slave by that name. If so, Commander Naaman would possibly be interested in him. It may be that this young man has significant value to the Commander."

"You should check with one of the soldiers to see if this slave is the Obid he is seeking." His wife continued with her duties as she talked. "Ah, my husband, when you return to the mines, see how many Obids you have working there. One might be the one he seeks."

"That's it!" her husband struck the table. "There have been questions asked by the soldiers if anyone knew of an Obid from Samaria. If anyone knew of such a one, they should report it to the First Legion." He rubbed his beard as he thought.

"Hmmm, I wonder if there is a reward of some type involved." As he went to bed that night, his last thought was how to report the news to the First Legion before anyone else realized the young man might be the one for whom Commander Naaman was searching. He decided to go through his list of slaves to see if there were other Samaritan Obids in the mines.

Was there reward money involved?

34

In the dark Hole, Obid and Ewslet did not speak for hours. Both were sitting hunched over, facing opposite sides of the well — for the "Hole" was a sort of well. The only light came from above, but it was now dark outside so only moonlight and a few stars showed overhead. It was so deep that there was no chance of escape, therefore, no guard stood on duty. The only good thing was that no rain had fallen lately, so they were not sitting in mud although the floor of the well was a bit damp.

Finally, Ewslet offered an apology. "I'm sorry. I did not mean it when I said girls from your village were ugly. I've never even met any girls from your village. I did not mean to talk against your sister for I do not even know what she looks like."

Silence.

Obid stretched out as much as possible on the dirt floor and said nothing. He was angry at Ewslet for talking about his village, the girls in his village, and especially his sister. His anger was mainly because it brought up memories of his family. He had tried to keep memories of his family and village in the back of his mind. Thinking about them made him too sad. Since the cave-in and his father's death, his anger at his situation grew.

He did not know where his baby brother might be. He had been busy trying to hold off the soldiers when he saw Amir across the horn of a huge horse. Thoughts of his sister really made him sad – whether Sheera was even alive, or a slave, or being raped and abused by one of those filthy-mouthed Syrian overseers. It had been years since he'd seen her, but Sheera was and always had been, in his opinion, one of the prettiest girls in his village and was to be betrothed to his best friend, Ari. Poor Ari; he had watched Ari die, so there would be no wedding for his sister, and who knew about the fate of his father from the latest mine cave-in.

He absolutely refused to discuss his sister with Ewslet while rotting in the Hole.

When the sentence was passed by Shobach, nothing was said about how long they would be in the Hole, whether they would be given water or fed that nasty gruel in the morning or even if they would be left there to die.

It was known that when slaves were placed in the Hole during the rainy season, some would drown. Others were down there so long that they were sometimes forgotten until too late. Unless another slave was placed in the Hole, no one would remember there were still two men inside. At least they had not been beaten by the overseers before being placed inside the Hole.

The Hole was a blessing instead of the beatings. When he first arrived at the mines, Obid had seen miners beaten to their deaths. The overseers had no mercy for slaves which caused trouble. Some lived afterwards and others were never seen again in his area.

He remembered seeing an albino slave who was called Aliabah by the men. Being deaf and unable to speak, he was unable to learn or speak the Syrian language and kept to himself. If a joke was told, he would only smile or nod his head. It wasn't long before they realized that Aliabah could not hear or speak, therefore sound meant nothing to him. The men used their hands and fingers to communicate with him and he would nod his head to signify that he understood. Mining was repetitious so there were no problems with the instructions. No one knew of Aliabah's nationality and it did not matter for they were all slaves.

One day one of the overseers asked him a question that he was unable to answer so the overseer believed he was being insubordinate. When the other miners tried to explain he was unable to answer, the overseer refused to listen to them.

Aliabah was dragged away and beaten so badly that instead of being a light-skinned man with reddish eyes, his entire body was red from the blood that came from the beatings. They could hear the bones breaking as he was struck by the overseer. The horrible beatings lasted for some time. The first swing of the club broke his jaw, the clubs had also broken his ribs, which punctured through his lungs. They could hear his cries late into the night, even after the beatings ceased. The keening sound was horrible.

Somewhere close to dawn, the men realized his screams had stopped — for Aliabah had died.

The slaves of each nationality in their section cried as they mourned him. The Israelites offered prayers for the dead man while praising Yahweh that the slave would not have to endure such torture ever again.

When the other overseers came to check on him, they found that Aliabah's bones had been so badly broken that the dead man was dragged away as a child's rag doll. The miners in his section mourned for the man who had never caused any problems or given any trouble to the overseers.

When the old slave master found out about Aliabah's handicap, the mean overseer was transferred to another area in order to keep peace among the other slaves and prevent an uprising. To appease the irate slaves, the old slave master served them a decent meal of meat and vegetables and they only worked a half day. The men barely ate the offering.

Within a fortnight, the old slave master was also removed and replaced by Shobach. Even though he was not a merciful man, Shobach really did not like the beatings for he found that he could only use healthy men in the mines. When he took over, his first change was to limit the beatings and the number of club strikes an overseer could use. However, he did not worry about the whippings. Men were still whipped, but never to their death.

One thing about being a slave in the mines — if one died, the raiders would just pillage another village to replace the dead one with one, two, or more. When Obid's village was raided, he and the other captured males became the ones to dig the dead miners out of their muddy graves and take their broken bodies to be burned. There were no graves for the slaves who died in the mines.

Following the latest cave-in, he thought he spotted his father on a stretcher, but could not be sure for it was dark. His eyes were closed. Was he sleeping, unconscious, or dead? Most of the young men he grew up with that had been placed in the mines along with his father and himself had either died in a cave-in or from injuries from beatings. Some were removed to the gold mines because the Syrians were afraid to keep families and villagers together to prevent problems.

And if the one on the stretcher was his father, was he being carried away alive or dead? The man's face was covered, his legs were wrapped and he had a make-shift sling on his arm. When he saw the man's body, he could only think, "all is not well."

When he asked one of the rescuers if they knew the names of those who were being brought out of the mines, the rescuer had replied that his job was to carry out the dead and wounded, and not ask who they were.

He gave some thought to Ewslet and his insults, realizing he may have started the argument by mentioning how beautiful were the women of his village. Ewslet responded by saying the females of his village were more beautiful than any other village and he had heard that Obid's village produced some of the ugliest women that Yahweh ever created. Then he started mocking Obid's mother and sister.

Obid loved his mother dearly and mourned with his father and sister upon her death. But the baby, Amir, brought the family joy. He hardly ever cried and always had a smile on his lips. Sheera took over the care of their baby brother as if he was her baby. The older women of the village offered to help raise him, but Sheera only allowed them to do minor things. His mother had been a beautiful woman and his sister took after her.

Calling his village's females and his sister ugly was a true insult and that started the fight. As he was more muscular and stronger, he soon balled up his fist and slammed Ewslet in the face and the other man retaliated. All the rage bottled up inside him was in that first punch. They fought for at least 10 minutes before the guards noticed. The force of their punches caused them to pummel each other and tumble into other miners and finally into the overseer and a guard.

Before they rolled into the tall muscular overseer, Obid vaguely saw the overseer watching the fight avidly with a smile on his face. More than likely, if they had not rolled into that fat slob, they probably would have been allowed to continue to use their fists, finish the fight, and return to their section of the mine. It was only because the stupid overseer thought the fighters would be whipped that he called for more guards to help him pull the two apart and took them to the slave master.

Obid was not dumb and realized that Shobach could easily have had them both whipped, but for some reason, possibly Yahweh's mercy, they were put into the Hole.

35

Shobach awakened to the smell of breakfast being cooked over the brazier. As he splashed water onto his chubby face and smoothed his greasy beard, his thoughts took him to Obid. Over an hour later, he arrived at his table to await the miners being brought from their living quarters. As the miners filed past, he remembered that he had placed the two fighters in the Hole. He called over the overseer and asked him to bring Obid and Ewslet to him.

The same guards from the day before and the overseer dropped a ladder rope into the Hole, had Obid and Ewslet climb to the top and proceeded to finish dragging them out. Both arrived in front of the slave master, but refused to say anything. When repeatedly questioned, Ewslet finally answered they had nothing to say and that their differences had been settled.

"Is that true or are you making that up?" Shobach asked Obid harshly. "I will not allow any more fighting."

"True," said Obid, and Ewslet nodded his head.

After being told to return to the mine, without talking the two men walked side by side to their work areas. Nothing was said about giving them food or water. After a few hours, however, an older slave brought the water bucket around to the miners and both were able to get their first drink of water for the day.

After hoisting his girth and pushing back, Shobach left his work table and went to find the soldiers of the First Legion. Commander Naaman's soldiers were not hard to find, for their armor and dress was a different color than the other soldiers. They stood straighter, carried their height well, and were considered dangerous to the city's people. Commander Naaman was big and tall and so were his soldiers.

No one crossed the Legionnaires or talked against them, for they were First Legion — the best soldiers and fiercest fighters in King Ben-Hadad's army. Some of them had gone with Commander Naaman to Samaria for one reason or another. He hoped it was to find some raiders so they could attack a few villages to replenish the supply of slaves to work the mines. Since the cave-in killed many of the miners, the dead miners needed to be replaced.

He located one of the Legion soldiers by the main fortress wall making his rounds. "Sir," he called, "Sir!" The soldier's horse stopped near Shobach and the soldier asked if he wanted to speak with him.

"I have a slave at the main silver mine by the name of Obid. I was told that if I knew of a slave from Samaria by that name I should inform a soldier in Commander Naaman's army. Would you give that information to the

Commander for me?" The soldier raised his lance and nodded; after Shobach finished giving him pertinent information, the soldier continued on his way.

Smiling, Shobach rubbed his hands together and returned to his table at the entrance to the mines. All he could think about was whether or not Obid might be the one the Commander was seeking.

"I wonder how much he's worth if he is the right Obid?"

36

"I believe I may have good news, my dear," Naaman told his wife a few night's later before the evening meal as he removed his armor. "I have been informed that Sheera's father and older brother may be alive. Do not tell her yet until I meet with them to make sure the reports I've been given are true. I have sent word around that if any of the Samaritan slaves with the names Elah and Obid are in the city to inform my soldiers. Since the names are Hebrew names, I want to make sure they are the correct Elah and Obid."

"So far there are three Elahs and two Obids. No word on a child named Amir, but something may come up later. I have already met one Elah, but he is not the right one. One of my general's is housing a slave by the name of Elah who was hurt in a cave-in at one of the silver mines a few months back. I will talk with him today. Meruru's slaves are taking care of this man in his healing rooms."

Mistress Tirah clapped her hands joyously. "That is very good. Sheera will be so pleased to find that some of her family might still be alive. She has been telling me about Yahweh and about the Prophet Elisha. She has given me a history of her people and has been showing me how to pray. We have been praying that her family is alive and well. We've also said special prayers to Yahweh for us."

Naaman turned to her and raised one eyebrow. "A special prayer for us, you say? What type of prayer?" The Mistress lowered her head as she blushed and whispered, "That we may become fruitful."

"Ah, Tirah, that it may be so." He hugged her to him and kissed the top of her head. "Perhaps in time, my dear, perhaps in time."

Naaman had taken the soil he brought back from Samaria and made a small altar in order to worship the God of Prophet Elisha. The altar was placed to the side of the compound near the grape house. He and his wife had been worshipping before the newly-made altar. He later allowed Sheera, Amram and Dahameen to know of the altar and worship there for they were Israelites who believed in the One God. A few of his Hebrew servants had traveled with Naaman to the Jordan and had helped to put the Samaritan soil on the mules to bring back to Damascus.

"I believe that your prayers will be answered and children will come." Naaman completed dressing, kissed her, called for Amram and left the room.

Tirah lowered her head and smiled to herself. She had just passed the second month of not having her monthly. She was afraid to say anything in the event she was not actually pregnant. Since her husband's return a few months back, she forgot to keep a record of her courses; but lately she has been feeling somewhat ill when she arose each morning.

Today she planned to talk to her servant and friend, Sunih, for Sunih was also a midwife to the Israelites. Tirah knew Sunih would keep her secret no matter what the outcome.

37

Commander Naaman walked with one of his First Legion soldiers toward General Meruru's home. Legionnaire Ab-Hiren gave Naaman information about the man, Elah, and information relayed to him about the two men named Obid.

"The Obid who works in the mines is a tough one. I see no problem with him, but according to the overseer, he is quite a fighter. I don't really trust the word of that overseer, for he is the only one with that report. Yet, the slave master, Shobach, says he never had a problem out of him or another one called Ewslet, until this past week. But I guess that episode is over, for they both work in the same mine area and seem to be getting along. I viewed them working side by side just yesterday. They don't talk to each other much, but are hard workers."

Naaman nodded his head thoughtfully as they were led into General Meruru's spacious quarters.

General Meruru saluted, smiled and shook hands with the Commander. The three men then walked outside of the house to a rear area. When they entered the slave quarters, there were only a few men inside, lying upon elevated mats.

The General approached his overseer, who turned and shouted, "Elah of Samaria!" Elah stood with the aid of a makeshift crutch and bowed low. Naaman could see his leg was wrapped with a wooden splint to keep the bone in place. He also saw a slight facial resemblance to Sheera.

"Sit, sit," ordered Commander Naaman, "I need to ask you a few questions about your family."

"Probably dead, my lord," replied Elah sorrowfully in Hebrew, then switched to Aramaic. "Our village was raided years ago. I have a son named Obid, who worked with me in the mine, but my area caved in. I'm not sure if his part of the mine was touched or if he survived. My youngest son, Amir, was taken captive during the raid, and I don't know the whereabouts of my daughter, Sheera, whether dead or slave."

Commander Naaman gave a wide smile and said, "I will personally check as to whether your family may be in the city. In the meanwhile, I would like to ask General Meruru if you are able to be transported to my compound in a few days."

He turned to the General who nodded his head. Meruru hesitated and then stated, "Elah is not my slave, but belongs to the mine area. I will get a release for him and my servants will carry him there the day after tomorrow. I understand his leg was broken, but is on the mend." Elah smiled in confusion as he stood to bow to the soldiers as they prepared to leave.

One hour later, Naaman, Meruru and Ab-Hiren were back in Meruru's house and had a short repast. "Thank you, General. I don't think I need to see the other Elahs, for I believe this man is the one I was seeking. Now to talk with the two Obids that Legionnaire Ab-Hiren has lined up for me."

Toward mid-day, Commander Naaman and Legionnaire Ab-Hiren had observed that the first Obid was a young man from Gilgal and could not be the one he sought. Too young and he was not from Aphek in Samaria. Immediately, they left that area and headed to the edge of the city toward the mines.

As they traveled to the mine area, a slave boy walked past them carrying a pack on his back that seemed to be very heavy, yet he carried it with a straight back. As the boy began to walk around the soldiers, he almost tripped, caught himself, and hoisted the pack to a better position. Ab-Hiren caught one end so that it did not drag and the boy smiled at him and thanked him in Aramaic.

Commander Naaman stared at him and put his hand on the boy's shoulder to halt him. The boy looked up quizzically and a little fearful.

"Don't worry, son," he said, "you look familiar. Do I know you?"

Again, in Aramaic, the boy answered him, "No, my lord, I don't believe so."

Naaman continued to study him. He could see he was a slave by the band around his arm yet his facial characteristics were the same as Elah's, only boyish. Could this be the younger son of Elah?

"Tell me boy, what is your name?" With his eyes to the ground, he answered, "I am Amir ben Elah of the village of Aphek in Samaria, slave to one of the King's soldiers, named Ranah."

Naaman gave a shout and turned to Ab-Hiren, "Ranah, one of the King's men. Yes, yes. Ab-Hiren, go to Ranah and tell him I have need of this slave. Purchase him if you have to. Come, young man, with me."

Amir looked around in bewilderment. "Yes sir, but I have to take this bag to the kitchens. The cooks are awaiting my return."

He stood first on one foot, then the other. Amir knew he did not do anything wrong and soldiers had never conversed with him before. What was happening?

Legionnaire Ab-Hiren and the Commander whispered together, then the soldier turned to Amir and said, "You and I will go together to Ranah's home and I will speak to him. You will pack your belongings and together we will go to Commander Naaman's home." Amir looked at him in disbelief. Commander Naaman! Everyone knew of this great soldier, who led many to victory in the Syrian wars. What could this mean?

The Commander continued on to the mines and as he walked another Legionnaire came forward to walk with him. Naaman told him the reason for his journey to the mines and the soldier left his post to another soldier and continued with him.

Amir's face showed uncertainty behind Ab-Hiren as they headed for Ranah's home. Even though his burden was heavy, adrenalin was allowing him to walk quickly as he pondered the reason for the move from his home.

Was he being sold? What would happen to him if he was sold? He knew the big man was a soldier of importance – much more important than Ranah. Could he be the Commander to whom Ranah reported? Even the soldier he was following was of a higher rank than Ranah for he could tell by the clothing.

He'd done nothing wrong, just doing his chores. But, what about Pridi? She was the only connection to his past and he had begun to consider her as his sister. What about Mahli's lessons for the day? If he didn't show, would Mahli have him beaten or whipped? His mind was in a jumble as he continued his steps.

38

Later that week, Pua and Shatii headed toward the riverbed to wash their personal clothing when a small open carrier passed by their area. On each side were two young men who looked straight ahead holding the poles effortlessly. A man was lying upon a pallet in the carrier with a make-shift crutch lying beside his wrapped leg. He turned his head and smiled when he saw them and lifted his arm in a short wave. Smiling, they waved back as they continued toward the river with their bundle of clothes. Shatii noticed the man's smile looked familiar, but shrugged her shoulders and quickly dismissed the man from her thoughts.

As the two reached the riverbed and joined other maids with their laundry, Shatii observed a handsome young servant standing guard over the women. "Pua, there is a new slave standing guard by the rocks to your right." Pua looked over and nodded.

"Yes, she replied, "he came some days' ago. I heard the Master tell him that his duties would be to watch over the areas near the kitchens, as well as the barns behind the house. I saw Amram giving him duties for inside the house early this morning and later saw Master Naaman talking with him again."

"It was strange, Shatii, but the Master had his hand on the man's shoulders as if he was whispering something to him. I understand from the house servants he has already been instructed to not go near the back area of the house. He is to be trained to be a bearer for the Master's carrier. Watching the servants wash clothes must be one of his other duties."

The two maids finished their observations and went back to beating their garments on the rocks and rinsing them in the flowing river.

39

Obid had risen early and watched the sun rise over the mountains. He thought back to almost three weeks ago when the Legionnaire came to retrieve him. Shobach was only too happy to bring him before the soldier and gave the widest of smiles when a bag of coins was placed into his hands. He had wondered if he had been released from the mines and was now the soldier's slave, newly sold to him, but the soldier explained that he was taking him to Commander Naaman's compound.

Obid remembered the large man, for he had answered questions from the Commander about his family, how their village was raided, and the fact that he had no idea where his family might be located following the raid. The Commander and the legionnaire soldier sat with him in a small tent outside of the mine area as he answered questions while the Commander stared intently at him.

Seeing movement outside the tent, he was able to see the shadow of Shobach's large frame hovering trying to listen to what was being discussed. When he looked at the tent's open flap, the Legionnaire turned and also noticed the slave master. The soldier stood and calmly walked over to the opening and slapped it closed, then stood with his back to it. Shobach quickly moved away from the tent's opening.

Obid had not wanted to talk about his family, for even though it had been years since he last saw them, it still made him very sad. Too many questions and answers about his village and family – first Ewslet, then Shobach, and then the Commander. He believed it was men such as the Commander and this Legionnaires that raided his village and brutally killed his family and friends.

After questioning Obid, the Commander told him he would not be going back into the mines. Someone would come for him later in the day and escort him to his compound. The big man walked with a military gait as the Legionnaire walked beside him. Obid felt it was best to not ask questions, but he was still confused about the events of the day.

Later that afternoon, the same Legionnaire returned and commanded him to walk with him away from the mines toward the middle of the city. He was taken to the rear of a very large home, shown a pallet in the middle of the slaves' quarters and was told he would be sleeping on the pallet in that section tonight. After the soldier left, Obid walked around the large room and seeing the 24 neatly arranged pallets, which meant 24 men slept there.

A smiling young slave, thin for his age with a green band around his arm, came in and placed a small plate of fruit, cheese and coarse bread on the pallet. There was also a gourd of fresh water that was not muddy brown. He was told in Aramaic that he would be given something more sufficient to eat later at the evening meal and hoped that the offering on the plate was sufficient. Still smiling, the slave turned and walked out of the room.

Obid looked at the fresh fruit and cheese and smiled. Sufficient! Since he was the only one there, the entire meal must be his. Quickly he grabbed the plate, sat cross-legged on the pallet, and began stuffing the wonderful food into his mouth.

Gobbling the cheese and gulping the water, he realized it had been a long time since he was able to have food brought to him on a plate. The water was clear and so good that he laid back on his pallet and sighed. And from the boy's words, he would be given another meal later in the evening.

40

A man who introduced himself as Dahameen came a bit later to explain his work details and then led him to the horse stalls. One of his duties would be to clean behind the horses until meal time. Dahameen showed him stable equipment and tools as he quietly explained that first thing in the morning another slave would take him on a tour around the compound and later to the river.

Another duty would be security and he would be shown where to stand guard over the women and girls who came to wash clothes. They have not had any problems with men going after the women and it is up to him to make sure this continues.

The man stood very regal as he gave instructions and when he finished, he nodded to Obid and touched Obid's shoulder on his way out of the stables.

Obid nodded and picked up a bristle brush to curry the horses. When he finished he began shifting the hay around and removing the dung to another area of the stables for disposal. The hay was clean – cleaner than the hay he slept on at the mines. It had been a long time since he had tended horses — and what beautiful animals they were too! The horses nuzzled him as he worked. It was so good to see something besides cave walls and mud!

Two slaves arrived and began to work on the roof of the stables. They looked at Obid and he looked back at them but none spoke as they all continued their work.

Food – decent food – was brought to him after sunset by a young slave with a gourd of water and a packet of clothing for him to wear in the morning. He went back to the same pallet he had been shown earlier. Other slaves began to arrive and looked at him for a few seconds, then readied themselves for bed, heading toward individual pallets themselves.

Obid opened the packet and looked the clothes over, placing them on the edge of his pallet. Previously in the mines he only wore ragged pants from the waist down, but the clothes he would be putting on in the morning were two pieces, a shirt-like vest and a type of short breeches of a coarse material.

Before the sun was up, he was awakened by slaves rising throughout the building. Obid found that he had slept very comfortably and it was good to not have to think about going to the mines. The other slaves showed him a small area for relieving himself and bathing which was closer to the slave barracks than yesterday's area.

As he slid into the water, he could feel his body giving a long sigh. "Aaahhhh!" The only washing he could remember since the raid was when the rains came and the mine workers were allowed to stay outside the caves when they flooded. Shobach didn't want the slaves to drown; he was always behind in his ore count and a drowned slave was a slave who no longer worked.

The cave and the men's body odors had become so common-place that hygiene failed to matter any more. The water felt so good and as he washed the dirt off himself, he began to feel cleansed inside and out.

Obid stayed in the pool so long that a few slaves had to come tell him it was time for him to work and not rest in the water. He was a slave and slaves had work to be done.

After performing his new chore of checking on the cattle and horses, he returned with the other men to the slave quarters for breakfast. Slowly they moved to their seating on the long benches and one man showed the new slave where to sit. On the long table were fruit, cheese, gruel and coarse bread. Obid practically shoved the good-tasting food into his mouth and gulped the water when he lifted the gourd to his mouth.

At one point it seemed the water went down his throat too quickly and he almost gagged. He didn't want to spit up the water for fear that it was his daily ration. Surprisingly, he was told to slow down by the other slaves for he would be allowed to have more than one gulp! When he realized the other slaves were watching him, he blushed.

One of the older slaves who sat next to him jokingly spoke in Sidonian, then changed to Aramaic, not knowing that Obid was able to understand him in either language.

"You do not have to eat and drink so quickly. We will all make sure you get more food tomorrow, and go easy on the water -- for no one will try to drink the entire bucket!" At first the man chuckled, then he laughed outright. Within seconds, the others laughed with him.

Obid then slowed his eating and drinking and closed his eyes as he savored the meal. This was not mine gruel for it contained dates and honey. He thought to himself, "Yahweh be praised!"

All of the slaves seemed to know he had just come from the mines and understood his hunger. "You will receive slave fare, of course, but I know this fare is probably much better than what you received in the hills. The Commander and the Mistress make sure all their slaves are fed adequately. You would not get this anywhere else in the city."

Obid nodded his head as he looked along the long wooden table. The other slaves nodded in the affirmative and he again silently thanked the Lord for the bounty as he continued eating.

Soon, the older man gave a signal and all of the men stacked their dishes to one end of the table and one by one began to leave to their separate duties.

41

Obid thought over what was said last night. The slaves told how they were captured or sold to this compound. One said he and five others were brought by his owner to the slave block because he was broke and needed the money and he was sold to the Commander.

The tall, big man said he had been a smithy in his village and the Commander was in need of one, so he was brought by a slave master to the compound. When Dahameen saw him, he had him work for three days to see if his work was good. After the three days, he was purchased. Since the Syrians are more advanced with metals and bronze, his work was easier here than in his village.

Another slave had introduced himself as an Ammonite and mentioned that he was supposed to have gone to the mines, but the Mistress was in the city shopping and saw that he was ill and feverish while he was being dragged by the raiders to get on the slave block. He said he would never think of being disloyal to this compound. It was the Mistress who purchased him to become one of her slaves and saved his life.

"She made the guards stop dragging me and saw that I couldn't stand on my own. She decided to make me one of her slaves and the raiders tried to ask for the same amount of money as if I was a healthy captive."

"She had Dahameen with her and when he looked at my bruises and the cuts, he whispered to her that I had been beaten by the raiders. That's when she told the guards that since I was too ill to work, why should she pay a large amount for a sick male? The Mistress purchased me for little or nothing. She's a bargainer, that woman!"

"I believe I would probably have been killed later for she was correct. After all a sick slave had no value so they released me to her. And when the raiders realized she was the wife of the Commander, a sold band was quickly placed on my arm. No money ever passed hands and unlike other slaves in this city, I was not branded with a hot iron to show ownership. I was allowed to rest for three days until I felt better before I was put to work. I owe the Commander's wife my life."

"She gave me over to the care of Dahameen, the Commander's head servant who was with her. He then turned me over to an older woman and another slave. Her slaves took me to General Meruru's slave quarters and I was nursed back to health.

When I was able, I was placed into the farmland area and now take care of some of the newborn and sick animals for both the Commander and General Meruru, who is under him.

"Dahameen is the compound's head servant, reporting only to the Master and Mistress. He handles the business and is over all the outside slaves. No one goes against him, for he has full power here. He is a fair slave master and if you do what you're supposed to do, you will never have a problem out of him. Whenever he has exacted punishment, it is because it was required like the slave who liked to touch the young women. If you have any problems, see Dahameen." All the men agreed.

Each man gave him information to him about the compound, the Master and Mistress, the families living here and what takes place on a daily basis.

"I praise the gods every day for allowing me to be here. I've been here over three years. You should know that other slaves are ill treated and do not have some of the freedoms this place allows us."

"The slaves here are seldom beaten or whipped. You have to do something really horrible to either be sent to the mines or killed. If you're not killed, Dahameen would probably be told to sell you to the Assyrians, who will beat or whip you. We've known some in the city who do not live long after being sold to the Assyrians."

"We're told there is a place outside the city where slaves are thrown off cliffs, used as spear practice for the soldiers, or burned alive. They never reach the slave block. One man who was captured with me tried to fight the raiders when we came into the city. He knew he was outnumbered but said he would rather die than be a slave. The men and boys from my village were made to watch as he received 15 hot metal brands on his chest and was then run through with the sword. The raiders do not put up with men or women who are worthless to them."

"There are very few Masters who do not brand for most think of slaves as cattle. If you are branded by one Master and you are sold, then you may have more than one brand on your body, sometimes two or three. There are slaves who have had five or more Masters and that many brand symbols burned into their skin. The Commander's wife does not allow branding either as punishment or ownership."

Each of the other slaves then introduced themselves and told him stories of how they came to be in the compound. A few were purchased from the slave block, a few came as spoils from a battle, some were born into captivity, and a few were purchased by the Commander or the Mistress. One man showed five brandings on his body from being sold or exchanged.

Obid had one brand from being placed in the mines. He and his father were branded a day apart. His father was still ill when he was branded, but both had the same symbols on their chests. To think, he would not be branded again as long as he was at this compound.

They each explained what their jobs were — a couple worked around the compound doing manual labor, a few worked in the grape room as well as in the field as vinedressers, or were makers of wine; some tended the farmland owned by the Commander, and some took care of the animals. Two were in charge of the Commander's battle equipment and armor of which, they said, there was an abundance.

When he asked about the slave who liked to touch the young women, they looked at each other and one quietly told him it was best not to ask. "He's no longer with us," came the reply.

42

Later that afternoon he was told that he would continue handling the horses and cattle, something he used to do in his village. Since Obid was tall and muscular, Dahameen returned to inform him he would also be trained in a few days to be one of the carrier bearers for the Commander's wife. The other carriers would train him and teach him how to maneuver around the city.

Dahameen was pleased to learn that Obid not only spoke Hebrew, but also Aramaic, Ethiopian, as well as Sidonian, Phoenician, and Gadara. He also has a grasp of two other languages, but that was because slaves from those areas worked in the mines with him. Having to work in the mines with other nations, Obid explained, it was easier to learn the languages of his work group in order to do the job correctly than to constantly misunderstand elementary hand signals.

In the beginning, the languages were confusing since one word could mean two or three words in some of the other dialects and other words that complimented in Hebrew was an insult in another. He had to admit it was good to work with Ewslet in the beginning because they were both Samaritans and there was no language barrier. Following the fight, however, they only spoke to one another when necessary, but as they later became friends they constantly used Hebrew.

Obid made sure he did not look at the women who were washing clothes. He did not want it construed that he was staring at them. Strange – if he was a slave, he was beginning to feel like a village chief after slaving in the mines. There was no overseer or guards to watch over him, and these slaves seemed like one big happy family. Last night and in the morning there was laughter and joking during the meal. At one point, his eating habits were joked about, but he knew it was in jest.

When the last of the women completed their wash at the river bank, Obid walked in front of them back to the house and left them in the rear of the building; he then turned right and headed for the barn.

The head slave, Dahameen was waiting for him in the stables to show him how to hitch and saddle the horses, and then explained what should be done to the wagons, chariots and drays. He also informed him of the slave rules, as to how he should act around the Master and Mistress.

"You will seldom see the Mistress," he stated, "but the Master likes to appear in the stables from time to time check on his horses. That big black one and the white one over there are his personal horses."

Obid stared at the coal black horse and the large white spotted horse to the left. Both horses turned their heads toward him and returned his stare. "Keep them well groomed and you won't have any problems."

Dahameen and Obid sat on one of the bales of hay as he warned him about which areas of the compound he should and should not go. "Whatever you do, don't sass another servant, and mind your manners! I've heard about your fighting. Don't try running away or stealing and you'll live to be an old man with your hands and feet intact," he admonished.

Obid had seen some of the slaves in the mine whose fingers had been cut off due to stealing and heard of those whose tongues were cut out from bad-mouthing their Masters, and was also aware of those who had been put to death. There were also men who had been beaten to the point of death, thrown off mountains, or even burned alive. The Syrian mines were not the only dangerous areas.

When he asked, Dahameen told him about the recent problem with a slave who was a good worker, but loved to touch the younger women. "That slave is no longer with us. You are replacing that young man so be very careful. You will be well treated and should know that you are privileged to be a slave in the household of Commander Naaman. He is strict and likes things just so, but he is also a good Master so treat him well and you will be treated accordingly. Any questions you may have, do not ask another slave. Ask me!"

Obid thought a while, remembering what the slaves had told him at the evening meal. Then he asked, "What happened to the slave who liked to touch the young women? The one I am replacing?" The older man looked him in the eyes and blandly repeated, "He is no longer with us." With that, Dahameen left the stables.

Obid found horse brushes, water and, stepping into the first stall, proceeded to groom the Master's horses. Later, when he was alone, he realized that Dahameen did not speak to him in Aramaic, but in Hebrew.

43

Sunih came from the rooms of Mistress Tirah with a smile on her face. A baby, she thought, we're having a baby! It will be so good to hear the voice of a child around this compound. It is good that the Master is now well and able to produce a child. Perhaps the baby will be a boy, for men tend to desire boys, even though their wives desire girls. A girl would be wonderful and give Mistress Tirah joy for when her husband goes off to wars. She had been lonely for too long. She was sure that no matter what the gender, the Commander and Mistress would love the baby.

Later in the afternoon, Sunih passed by Tirah's private quarters to check on her new gowns which had been delivered from the spinning room. Risa was doing a wonderful job on the Mistress' new clothes. Her skills were expanding and she had begun creating new patterns and designs she remembered her mother used to sew. She, Shatii, Pua and Sheera were collaborating on new fashions for the Mistress. Soon Sunih would have to tell the girls they would have to begin making looser garments as the Mistress expanded. As she headed toward the rear of the quarters, Tirah gaily called to her.

"Oh Sunih, I am so happy; I just want to tell everyone! My husband and I worried that we would never have any children and now I am pregnant!" Tirah walked around the room beaming from ear to ear and then came to a halt in front of the older woman. Happily, Tirah reached out and put her arms around her neck and gave her a great hug. Somewhat surprised, Sunih enthusiastically returned the hug. Then she put her hands on the Mistress' shoulders, setting her back a few inches and looked her straight into the face. She tried to speak her words cautiously.

"Mistress, I don't want to alarm you, but I think you should wait at least another month before saying anything just now. Your husband should be the first person to announce your pregnancy before the gossip spreads through the compound, but please wait another month. Pregnancies are sometimes difficult, but if Yahweh wishes it, you will be all right. Let's just wait a bit more."

Tirah put her head down and nodded in agreement for she knew there were always risks in having babies. But that did not daunt her. "Amram and Dahameen told my husband that Yahweh does not do things halfway so I know all will be well with me." It was no surprise that Tirah was excited.

Tirah patted her stomach and looked into the fruit bowl on the small table in her room. "I don't know what is wrong with me, Sunih, but I have a great taste for sugared dates. Would you see if the kitchen has any?" Tirah hadn't started to swell as yet but Sunih knew this would be happening.

She left her Mistress and headed toward the kitchen area to fulfill her wishes. For some reason, she just knew all would go well with Tirah and her pregnancy.

As soon as Sunih had confirmed Tirah's pregnancy, she had consulted with some of the midwives in the compound. Knowing they would not tell anyone, they had agreed to keep the Mistress' pregnancy quiet until Tirah waited another month and informed the Commander. One thing Sunih knew about midwives, for she was one herself, they kept pregnancies a secret until the woman began to blossom.

Sunih was so happy that the great Prophet Elisha had healed the Master. She had never met the prophet, but knew Yahweh caused this to be. Still smiling, she went to the back of the house and headed outside to watch the house servants go about their duties. There seemed to be an air of happiness around the compound today.

As she stood there in the doorway, a boy touched her on the arm to ask directions to the kitchen. "Please help me find the kitchen. I was shown how to get there the other night but this morning I seem to be lost. This house is much larger than the one I previously worked in."

Sunih looked at him and said, "Follow me for I am on my way there myself. I've never seen you before — and who might you be?" The young man bowed before her and said, "I am Amir ben Elah of Aphek in Samaria and am newly made a slave here as of a few days ago."

Amir noticed her clothing was not the usual servant's robe, but a light green of a soft cloth, similar to the slaves he remembered from the previous weeks who walked beside the carrier with the beautiful lady. The servants in this household have nicer clothes than what was worn at the soldier Ranah's house, he thought. Following the older woman, they made their way to the kitchen.

Hmmm, Sunih thought, Amir! Just this morning, Mistress Tirah had told Sunih about Sheera's family and the fact that her husband had been trying to find her brothers. Ever since Sheera told the Mistress about the Prophet Elisha and the Master had undergone his miraculous healing, the Master was trying to repay her for her help.

She knew Elah was now established in the servants' quarters in the rear of General Meruru's compound and that his son, Obid, was to have arrived a few weeks ago. She had not seen Obid as yet, but could see the family resemblance of Amir, Sheera and Elah.

Mistress Tirah had confided in her that there was to be a secret reunion of the family in a week to ten days. Her husband was waiting a little longer for Elah's leg to heal.

Sunih patted him on the shoulder and led the way to the kitchen area. She pointed out corner beams and showed Amir how to look for landmarks around the building that would keep him from losing his way.

"This house is quite large, but you will soon get used to it. If you lose your way again, just ask any of the servants." Upon reaching the kitchen, she introduced Amir to the kitchen servants and left him.

Sunih traveled slowly from the house to General Meruru's area and then to the servants' quarters; she then headed toward the rear of the building. Elah was sitting on the side of an elevated pallet and her grandson was bowed before him dressing his leg.

"Ah," she said as she looked on. "I see your leg is healing quite well, Elah. You were lucky the mine did not cave in on your leg shattering the bone into pieces." Elah stood and tentatively put his weight on the leg that had been in the splint.

"Your grandson, Jesse, is quite a healer. Ever since he and another carried me out of the mine, he has taken great care of this leg, coming to see me every day, changing my bandage and making me exercise it a little each day. He was ever so careful in taking me from the mines and bringing me here to General Meruru's. His skill has my collar bone mended and he was there during my fevers. You should be very proud of him, Sunih. I will soon be moving to Commander Naaman's quarters."

"Humph!" Sunih hugged her grandson and admonished him to get back to his duties. "Mistress Petra will be ready to go to the marketplace, Jesse, for today is her shopping day and you are needed to help with her carrier. Don't get yourself into any trouble by staying away too long."

Jesse stood, flexed his back and arms for a second, then leaned over and kissed his grandmother. "I'll check on you again this evening, Elah, to see how you fare without the splint on your leg. Don't try to move too fast and fall over. Get your leg used to walking normally. I refuse to treat your leg any more." He gave his grandmother a quick wink, laughed and strode away, saying "I know, Omah, I know. I will not be late for I have time!" Elah and Sunih watched him leave and both had smiles on their faces.

"He is a great man, Sunih," Elah said.

"I know," she replied, "he is a blessing to me. His sister worked for Commander Naaman's wife as her personal maid. She was sickly and died a time ago. Everyone loved her; I loved her, but Yahweh loved her more. There is another maiden in her place that reminds me of her." Sunih spoke with Elah for a few more minutes then started to leave.

Elah halted her and said, "I don't know why Yahweh has favored me to come here, but I thank Him for how He has cared for me and brought me in contact with you and your family. Thank you, Sunih, and also a big thank you to Jesse. I have prayed Yahweh's blessings on Commander Naaman and his wife. Living here for these few months has been a true gift from God."

"Commander Naaman is allowing me to work on the farm where I can use my skills to grow fruits and vegetables. I even went hunting the other day and even though I sat on the ground, I caught two ducks with my bow and arrows. Another slave takes me to the fields with him in a dray and then brings me back. This is the first time of my captivity that I feel like Yahweh has once again smiled on me. I am truly blessed." Elah felt like crying, but held back his tears until Sunih had left the room."

What is wrong with me, he thought. I am so grateful and yet I cannot stop the tears. Silently he praised Yahweh and asked Him to bless the Commander, General Meruru, their families, and all the slaves he had met since coming to Meruru's healing quarters. Soon he would be moving into the slave barracks at the Commander's compound. He had already met some of the Commander's slaves and knew the transition would be easy.

It was at this point that he made up in his mind that he would stop thinking about the mines. Even though he missed many of the men he worked with, he would try to remember only the men and not the experience.

44

Obid walked past the area of the house by the kitchens and heard whistling. He could tell it was a young man who was whistling. He smiled to himself as he thought back to how his baby brother struggled to learn how to whistle. He would purse his little lips and make tweeting noises, trying to get a whistle out of his mouth. Before the raid, Amir had started whistling in bits and pieces but could not hold the sound for a long period of time. Sometimes he and his little brother would walk the women to the riverbed and try whistling different tunes to each other.

It had been his plan to teach Amir how to make bird whistles; however, after the raid, he knew it would never happen. By now, Little Amir would have learned how to whistle he thought. That is, if he were alive and well. What he wouldn't give to walk with his younger brother and blow tunes together. There was no reason to whistle now, for whistling a song was a happy sound. He shook his head to clear the thought, but continued his walk to the slave quarters by the stables.

During the Jewish high holy days, all the Israelite servants were now able to observe the Jewish ceremonies in their slave quarters, with Amram and Dahameen serving as priests -- for they were from the tribe of Levi. They kept the traditions that had been handed down by their father. Since the Commander and Mistress now worshipped Yahweh, the religions of the slaves were relaxed for them to worship their own gods within the compound. In fact, even those slaves and servants who previously did not worship Yahweh would sometimes attend with them; a few had even converted.

Other slaves were also allowed to worship their own gods, including Rimmon, the god of the Syrians. Some of the newer slaves worshipped the sun, moon and nature, and they stayed within their own group.

45

The Mistress sat with Sheera and explained how Dahameen ran home to inform her of her husband's healing by the Prophet Elisha. Mistress Tirah said she was happy with the news, but until she heard the entire story from her husband, she was afraid they still might not be able to produce any offspring. She said at first she had many questions. How far did her husband's healing go? Was the healing only for her husband's skin? Did it include her husband's ability to produce a child, or even if the new God they worshipped would allow her womb to carry a child?

This morning, however, the Mistress joyfully informed her that she was to have a baby. And that Sunih has guessed that the birth would take place in less than five or six months. The Master was exuberant upon hearing the news. Sheera told the Mistress she was very happy for her and they enjoyed a very pleasant visit together.

Within a week of returning from Samaria, the Master and Mistress had met with Sheera and related the story of the Master's healing. They expressed their gratitude to her for telling them about the Prophet Elisha and his healing powers. Mistress Tirah said they were so very grateful they wanted to reward her with a home of her own so that when she married, she and her husband would have somewhere to live close by.

Sheera was not worried about that aspect for none of the Commander's slaves appealed to her. She did, however, have some feelings for one of the Hebrew slaves in General Meruru's compound. He would sometimes stop to talk to her when he brought Mistress Petra to visit with Mistress Tirah, for he was one of Petra's carriers. His name was Jesse. Jesse always made a point of coming to see her, yet used the excuse that he was looking for Sunih whenever he came to the house. She was later informed by the other slaves that Sunih was his grandmother.

She began hoping the Commander would not betroth her to someone she did not know or want. She knew that love had nothing to do with becoming betrothed as a slave. The Master or mistress could place a couple together simply to produce children, who would also be slaves for them. Of course, there were some female slaves who were given husbands by their Masters and later learned to love them. She felt Ari would have made a good husband, but that was when she was a free person and her family would be around for her wedding celebration.

After hugging her, the Master and Mistress rejoiced at his new physical state and the women cried tears of happiness. Of course, Master Naaman did not show his tears, for he stood to leave as he explained there was work to do and left the room, leaving most of the crying to his wife and her maid.

46

Sheera performed little of her duties today for she was given a strange assignment. Mistress Tirah called Sheera to her during late morning. "General Meruru's wife has asked for some special bowls for the servants that are ill and I would like you to take them to her. In the rear of the house is a section for ill or wounded slaves and the bowls should be carried to the General's compound. Dahameen will escort you there." Sunih had come into the room as the Mistress explained the assignment and gave her the bowls.

"Do not be afraid of the men in that area of the slave quarters, for the sick ones will be in another area and all the other male slaves will not be there during the day as they will be performing most of their work away from General Meruru's house. Dahameen will be with you to lead you to the General's house. And Sheera, change into your pale green robe, the one you and the others wear for special assignments. It looks so nice on you and the slave who will meet you was told he will know you by the robe's color."

As she began to leave the bundle with Sheera, Sunih had a very pleased smile on her face. Then she leaned over and hugged her. Sheera thought she heard her whisper something in Hebrew, which ended with the word 'Shalom.'

Strange, thought Sheera, why would the Mistress want me to carry these bowls to General Meruru's slave quarters? The male servants generally carry out assignments such as this. Besides, why send Dahameen with me as my escort and bodyguard instead of just giving him the bowls and having him give them to the General's slave overseer? You're a slave, she thought, just do as you're told! Thoughtfully she continued to walk behind Dahameen, trying to pace her steps with his.

She liked Dahameen very much for she was able to discuss many things with him in Hebrew. His brother, Amram, was Master Naaman's personal valet and the two of them were so much alike. Both men treated her, Shatii and Pua as their nieces, which the three loved for all considered them as family.

She learned that Dahameen and Amram spoke many languages, and when they discussed personal business in front of the slaves, would sometimes switch to another language. They lent an air of tranquility to the slaves and servants, even though they were over them.

Now here she was walking with Dahameen through the small alleys that supposedly, was a short cut to General Meruru's house. She had been to the General's house many times when her Mistress would go to visit his wife and they always took a different route. Perhaps, she thought, it was easier for the bearers to maneuver Mistress Tirah's carrier – still, this short cut seemed to take much longer.

Her guide was humming a song she remembered her father used to hum and sing when she was younger. Her thoughts ran back to Amir and how he loved to hear their father sing that same song as he tried to get his father to sing or hum it until he fell asleep. Her father always ended the song with "Yahweh is good and all is well."

Smiling, she continued on while thinking she would be able to visit with Aleea, who was now a maid for General Meruru's wife, Mistress Petra.

47

Obid searched the crowd for Dahameen and the slave girl with a pale green slave robe. He wondered why the Commander's women wore the pale green. They didn't even look like slaves in that color. However, his assignment was to watch for them, not worry about slave colors; take the bowls from the girl and walk with them to the rear slave quarters where some of the men who had been ill resided behind General Meruru's house.

He had been to the General's house many times since he began working in the Commander's household, taking messages and bundles since he arrived almost a month ago. Strange, he thought: Dahameen has free reign to go into all the slave quarters of Commander Naaman's generals and could easily take the bowls himself. Why send a female slave? That was asking for trouble — for if any of the men dared to touch the girl, problems would arise.

As he slowly gazed through the crowd, he saw Dahameen's straight form in the distance coming toward him, and a wisp of pale green material behind him.

In the mines, the men had one job – mine the silver or gold, dig and shovel. But being a slave in a household was different and he felt slaves performed some of the most foolish services. He had to admit that he never knew that there were slaves who were given free time or that they were not always beaten for any reason. He was grateful to be out of the mines, grateful to be a slave in the Commander's household, clean, fed decent food, and could make friends again.

Some of the other slaves had told him about the slave who was beaten by other slaves for touching a female slave girl. That slave was quickly eliminated from the household. Beaten? Hand cut off? Killed? Sacrificed? Sold? He doubted the slave was sold, for the next owner would surely not trust him around females. Perhaps he is now working in the mines. Of course, there was always the chance that he was killed when he was removed from the compound.

Obid was no fool and knew that slaves could be purchased for sacrifice as well as for work. But most sacrifices were of slaves who had great physical power, not of those who committed crimes. Criminals were generally put to death by torture, beheading, hanging, or by sword or spear.

He had watched the exchange of money from the Legionnaire's hands to Shobach's when he left the mines. He was now the property of the Commander and worked also with some of his generals, but especially with General

Meruru as he was today. He shook his head to clear that thought and realized he should walk toward Dahameen and the slave girl so he could lead them both to the slave quarters.

48

Sunih called Amir from the rear of the kitchen for he was placing pottery on the shelves under the direction of one of the head kitchen servants. As the boy ran toward her, she thought of her grandson, Jesse. When he was a young lad, he also would run toward her when she called.

Young Amir was biddable, full of life and loved to work beside her. He had told her he never knew his mother or grandmother, and she believed he was probably using her as a substitute.

Amir had met Jesse and since Jesse called Sunih 'Omah,' the Hebrew word for 'grandmother,' Amir sometimes caught himself calling her Omah. Whenever she went to the spinning room, he would take it upon himself to escort her there and back. She always felt safe in the compound for she knew all the slaves, but allowed him to stand guard for her at the door because he felt it was his duty.

She quickly developed a relationship with the young man and in one of their private discussions he told her of his capture. "Is there anything you miss since leaving the service of Ranah?"

Amir thought about the question for awhile and slowly answered, "Not really. I'm doing pretty much the same work here as I did for Ranah. I hardly saw Ranah for he is a soldier and works on the wall as a guard in the King's palace. If he was able, he would come home around mealtimes to eat with his sister. He loves Mahli – that's his sister. When I first arrived, I was almost a playmate for his sister, for she is only eight or nine years older than me, but acts like a child. As I grew older, she wanted me to be her teacher for she wanted to learn Hebrew and I was still learning Aramaic. We worked together with the languages. Her brother allowed it because he spoils her."

"But Mahli has a mean streak and throws tantrums, but she has never thrown a tantrum because of me. Once two slaves – a Moabite and an Ethiopian -- were too slow in removing some heavy items from her room and she had them beaten. Many of the slaves had been sick and some died. Those two had been sick and were not completely well. She knew the furniture was heavy, but made them do it because she said they should still be able to move the heavy stuff. It was my plan to help them for they were not well, but she made me leave the room. She didn't care about their health, just that they complete the work quickly. I think the fact that she could do as she wished gave her a certain amount of power over the slaves that took care of her."

"It is known among most slaves that General Meruru and his wife are a few of the slave owners who have set up healing rooms behind their houses for slaves that are sick or injured. Some slave owners will have their most trusted slaves sent there when they become ill. The Commander's slaves and General Meruru's slaves are well treated. Ranah reports to the General, and could send his sick slaves there, yet he never sends any to the healing room. If a slave dies, he just buys another one to take his place."

"I don't miss being in Ranah's household, but I do miss my friend, Pridi. She and I grew up together, although I'm a bit older. But she is the only link I have to my village since I have no family. Pridi works in Ranah's kitchen. She told me that she was in another soldier's household, but was sold to Ranah because she was not needed. We are of almost the same age, but she's very small, you see. She is comfortable there, but I'm afraid that if she does something wrong, Mahli will have her beaten as well. Luckily, Mahli does not travel to the kitchens very often, but if Pridi's duties change, she may have contact with her."

Amir was a likeable boy and the younger children of the slaves had started following him around the compound when their duties were over. Many times she caught Amir heading toward a small dirt area in the back of the compound. She followed him one day and at first she thought he was watching the little ones, but later realized he was educating. If he had no assignments for a time, while their parents worked, the boy would have a crowd of children under five or six sitting in a circle, sometimes playing games or teaching. He would make a great teacher when he reached an older age, she thought.

Sometimes he taught language skills, and other times he taught about Yahweh or Jewish history. She felt it incumbent to inform the Mistress because not all of the children were Israelite, and if such teaching took place in any other household, the slaves would be forced to worship the pagan gods. Even before his healing, the Commander allowed other religious worship by his slaves, but not within the compound. The Commander found that slaves and servants worked much better if allowed to worship their own gods.

So there would not be any problems about this new activity, it was best to report it. But when she was informed, the Mistress allowed it and soon began to sit near the children to watch and listen to Amir.

For such a young man, he was very knowledgeable of his history and his God. However Amir explained to the Mistress that he had learned a lot from his father and the Prophet Elisha when he was younger, as well as from the other Israelite slaves in Ranah's household.

Amir loved the Mistress and Sunih had observed that his love was returned. Now that she was pregnant, it was easy to see that Tirah might be hoping for a baby boy.

49

Sunih was standing in the doorway to the kitchen and found Amir heading toward her. She called to him to follow her to the side of the kitchen door.

"Amir, I need you to go to General Meruru's house and pick up some bowls from Dahameen and one of Mistress Tirah's servants there. They will be in the quarters behind the General's house where the ill men are situated. You will know her by her pale green robe," Sunih instructed.

"When you meet Dahameen and the girl, there should be another slave with them and you will lead them all toward the slave quarters in the rear of the General's compound. You've been there before, so you should have no trouble leading the three of them there." Amir understood and repeated the assignment to make sure he had it right.

"I have seen the girls with the pale green robes. They look very nice, Omah, not like other slaves," he said. After Sunih nodded her approval, he turned from her and went out. It is funny, she thought, Amir did not realize that the Mistress' maids were the only ones who wore the pale green robes when they went out with her. Otherwise the maids wore their tan robes inside the household. Sunih gave a broad smile and went back into the spinning room to complete her instructions to the slaves. They were beginning to make clothes, blankets, and robes for infants.

50

There was a new girl in the spinning room who had never spun linen or silk and had to be taught the use of the Syrian looms. Silk had been purchased from the traders and it had to be spun for curtains for the Master and Mistress' new quarters.

Rafeerah-Nob had been purchased by Mistress Tirah over a month ago but was healing from a whipping she received on orders from her previous owners. The Mistress was in her carrier on her way to the market and was furious to see the slave girl in torn clothing being punished in front of men in the center of the city. Most slave owners beat or whipped their servants in their home areas away from public view, or in the sight of other slaves as an example to them. But for a female slave to be whipped in the square was horrible.

The Mistress quickly approached the overseer and questioned why she had to be whipped. She then purchased the girl for a few coins. She instructed the overseer to tell his Master that the girl died during the whipping and that he should keep the coins for himself. The overseer thanked her and told her he doubted he would have any problems with his Master. He really did not want to whip the girl anyway, especially in the square, but he had to do as he was told. The Mistress directed one of her maids to lead the girl home to be handed over to Aweh.

When Aweh saw the bruises and marks on the slave girl, she washed her welts and attended to her other wounds. Aweh saw three brandings on the young flesh, one of which looked to be recent. When she asked if she had been in the service of three owners, Rafeerah-Nob said she was first branded by the head servant when she was purchased, but the owner branded her again a few years later and once again recently, because he didn't feel the first two were done correctly and wanted her to know to whom she belonged. She said she knew he just wanted to let her know who was Master, for he was a mean man and loved to see the pain he was able to inflict upon his slaves.

She was also able to glean from the girl that her Master wanted to have sex with her whenever his wife was away, but she refused and this time she fought back, making a large scar on his face with her nails. When his wife came home and saw the bleeding scar, he made up a lie about her that his wife believed. The angry owner then told his slave overseer to whip her in the middle of the city for her disobedience.

She admitted the overseer understood her plight and did not want to use the whip for he felt sorry for her, but overseers do as they are told. He knew of other female slaves who would give in to the Master's whims to keep from being beaten. He was aware that two young slave girls had been impregnated by him, but the Master sold them to another owner so the girls and their babies would not be in his household.

The girl told her she was given the Syrian name of Rafeerah-Nob by her owners, but her real name was Risa from a village near Mizpah. She was taken captive by the Syrian soldiers during a raid and was sold to this harsh Master and mistress when she arrived in Damascus. As she grew older and more developed, the Master began to lust after her. He would call her to his rooms whenever his wife went to market or visit friends and try to fondle her. She was given the whipping because she fought back with her nails and bit his shoulder when he tried to lie on top of her. In trying to get away, her robe was torn. Angry and frustrated, her Master made up a lie for his wife to believe and then ordered her away to be whipped.

"The overseer was also a slave but it was his job to whip me." She winced as Aweh washed her arms. "He tried not to be harsh, but the whip had its own mind. He had only given me a few lashes when the pretty lady saw me. When the woman offered to purchase me, he gladly sold me for a few coins."

"I overheard the lady tell the overseer to lie to his Master that I had fallen to the ground after the whipping, so he would presume I had died there in the square. He was to say that he had noticed someone leaning over me, but did not stay to see what was done with my body. I guess his Master would probably be satisfied with that answer for his wife would not want me to return to their house. He'll probably go to the square tomorrow and purchase another young girl."

Risa was stiff and sore, but happy to have someone to talk to. She told Aweh, "You're the first person to touch me with kindness." Risa sniffed a bit and then began to cry. Aweh looked at her with compassion and put her arms around the girl as she sobbed into her shoulder. "You will be safe here," she murmured into the girl's ear, then continued ministering to her wounds and bruises.

She opened to Aweh about her village, how the raiders killed many of her family and friends, sold some as slaves on the way, and the rest were sold in the square. There was sadness in her voice as she told Aweh of the village's burnings. She said she knew how to spin wool, but was not familiar with Syrian materials. She had just started working on materials when her Master put her out.

"My family's specialty was to make the dyes for the village. My mother and aunts taught me which plants and soils to use to create the colors of Yahweh's rainbow. I was not as experienced then as I am now, but since being a slave, I had begun to experiment with the flowers and herbs found here. I loved mixing the plants to make beautiful blues and yellow dyes and was showing some of the other slaves how to do it."

"I feel so badly for the other slave girls. The Master likes them young – very young. Being a slave means to answer to the Master's every whim; you could not say NO. The mistress was not so bad. She really had no control over us and just did as she was told. The only difference between her and the rest of us was that she could come and go as she pleased. My mistress had never been a slave, but her husband treated her like one. She was much younger than her husband."

"Once I watched him hit her because she talked back to him about something. He became very angry and hit her so hard she broke some of the pottery behind her and carried the bruises for over a week. He claimed he was sorry, and tried to comfort her, but I could tell it was not the first time he'd hit her in anger. Her only rest from him was to visit with friends and shop, which she did quite often."

A few days later, Sunih came into the room and started putting a healing salve on the girl's back and left arm. The skin around her recent branding was healing quite well on the back, yet the arm would continue to show the welts to remind her of her whipping. Sunih felt the name 'Risa' was better suited to the young girl and explained to the other slaves and spinners she was to be called Risa from now on.

Today was the first day she would be permanently situated in the spinning room and they would work together until she was proficient. Sunih decided to start with the wool skeins before working on the other materials. If there was a problem, it would be easier to take wool apart and re-do it than to re-do material. They trained together for a few hours and stopped for the mid-day meal.

As she headed for the kitchen to put together the Master and Mistress' meal, Sunih felt her talk with the new slave girl produced a thought, but it had quickly left her memory. The Commander had recently returned from the King's presence and would be home in the early afternoon to take his midday meal with his wife. Since the couple would eat their meal together, Sunih brought out the special tableware the potters had recently delivered and added extra dates and nuts into a flowered bowl.

Sunih put the food on the tray and headed for the front of the house. She saw Pua heading down the hallway and just as they met halfway, Pua asked Sunih if she needed any help. The older woman smiled and answered she could handle it, but asked if the maid would please push aside the curtains to the eating area for her. As she did so, Pua questioned if she would be needed in the spinning room following the meal?

"No, child," Sunih answered. "We have a new spinner who is being trained now to do some of the spinning. You, Sheera and Shatii will probably have some free time until she learns to work the treadles. Once Risa learns that, then the four of you will work together in a few days or so. Risa also knows how to make dyes, which would be helpful to us. She'll be able to show us some new colors soon."

"Risa?" Pua's eyebrows went up a bit as she continued her trip down the hallway. Her thoughts went to a conversation she had with Sheera when they first came to work for the Commander and his wife. She believed a captive by the name of 'Risa' was also in the trek from Samaria to Damascus. The young girl and Sheera had stayed together for the better part of the long migration. She believed Risa was in the slave line along with herself, Sheera and Shatii, but was one of the first to be sold.

She thought she would mention the name to Sheera the next time they were together. But within a few hours, she forgot about the new girl.

Sunih began laying the table with the meal when it occurred to her that perhaps it would be prudent to mention Rafeerah-Nob to Mistress Tirah.

Commander Naaman led his wife to the inner room and smiled at Sunih. After exchanging greetings with the two, Sunih whispered to the Mistress, "I have something to tell you; it's about the new slave girl."

Mistress Tirah smiled and said, "Don't worry Sunih, my husband knows I've purchased another maid for the spinning room. I thought it was best to let him know how I obtained her. You may tell us both."

Hesitantly, Sunih told them that the new slave was healing well and mentioned her brandings and the welts on her arm. At this, the Mistress nodded and said it was understandable. "I think you might be interested to know that Rafeerah-Nob's real name is Risa. The slave owner's wife gave her the name of Rafeerah-Nob when they purchased her because they wanted her to have a Syrian name."

Commander Naaman hesitated from eating and questioned her, "Are you sure her name is Risa?" Sunih nodded in the affirmative. Mistress Tirah looked at him strangely and he reminded her of the friend Sheera had discussed with her. "Remember, my dear, a girl named Risa was the first slave sold off the female slave block when they arrived in Damascus. Could that girl be her friend Risa?"

The Mistress asked Sunih if the new maid was able to walk from the slave quarters to her small inner room. Sunih nodded yes and said she would bring her to the room following the meal. The Commander said he would also be there to talk with the girl but it would be a quick talk. He and the Mistress had to be at General Meruru's later this afternoon.

51

Obid met Dahameen toward the center of the square and barely glanced at the slave girl behind him. When he heard a gasp from her, he turned around.

"Sheera! Sheera, is it you?" Almost knocking Dahameen aside, they ran to each other, hugged, and began to sob. Sheera was still holding tightly the bowls she was to deliver.

"Obid, oh Obid! Yahweh be praised!" Dahameen stepped politely to the side and waited while the reunion took place and felt he wanted to cry also. The people in the square barely glanced at the two servants and continued walking toward their destinations.

Amir saw a bit of commotion as he headed toward General Meruru's house and saw two servants hugging and crying while Dahameen stood to one side. Curious, he moved closer and saw the light green robe of a servant girl who must work for Commander Naaman, for that was the color they normally wore when they left the compound. He was almost on top of the two huggers when he realized that the girl in the green was his sister.

"Sheera? Sister? Is that you?" he cried.

Sheera turned and saw her baby brother, who was no longer a baby. "Obid, it is Amir! Obid, look, Amir!"

Obid turned to the boy and both stared at each other for a hesitant second, then almost collided with each other in a great hug. Once again the people in the square stopped to watch this new reunion. The three gave one great hug and continued to sob.

Dahameen began to think he was becoming a cry baby as well. First, crying with the Commander on his healing, and now crying with this family. He kept his head turned for some time, then cleared his throat with a great "harrumph" and said, "We have a duty to perform; let us get to it."

Dahameen led the way with the three family members following behind. All laughed when they realized that their Master and mistress were Commander Naaman and Mistress Tirah. Even though all worked in the same household, they realized they had never crossed paths. They also realized their owners must have had a reason for it.

The family kept walking toward General Meruru's house with their words tumbling over each other. Obid tried to explain about the mines; Amir was talking about being taken to Ranah the soldier's home; and Sheera was trying to explain how she came to be in the household of Commander Naaman and his wife.

Upon reaching General Meruru's home, Dahameen continued walking on a thin footpath toward the slave quarters in back of the compound with the three family members chatting and laughing behind him.

As he walked into the barracks section for ill or injured slaves, the three watched as a tall man with a slight build slowly began to stand beside his raised pallet.

52

Elah heard people coming toward his section of the slave quarters. He'd had quite a few visitors these past few months: the owner of the slave quarters who was named General Meruru, Ab-Hiren the Legionnaire, who led Commander Naaman, a high-ranking officer of the Syrian king, two well-dressed slaves named Dahameen and Amram from the Commander's household, the handsome young slave named Jesse, who brought him to these quarters and doctored his broken leg, and Jesse's grandmother, Sunih.

And now more people were coming to his section of the barracks. These were young voices of various timber approaching and their voices were jubilant.

He slowly began to stand by the pallet and carefully put his weight on the leg that Jesse had recently unwrapped from the splint. Now standing tall, he looked up and observed a young lady who closely resembled his dead wife, Relana, dressed in a pale green robe. Next to her a tall muscular young man with a small mustache and beard on his chin with one hand on the shoulder of a smaller muscular version and they were all coming toward him.

As he stared at them and they stared back at him, the realization set in that these people were his children. All three looked at each other then ran toward the man.

"Father!" The word was repeated by three different voices and then four voices were heard crying and sobbing. Elah could not believe it. His children were alive and well!

As he held out his arms, the three ran to him and each encircled his frame. Together the four sang laughingly, "Life is good and all is well." There was nothing they could do but laugh and sob. Elah, Obid, Sheera and Amir's words tumbled over each other as each tried to tell how they thought the others dead from the raid.

Dahameen silently walked toward the family, reached into their midst and slowly removed the bowls from Sheera's hands. Quietly he backed out of the slave barracks, leaving them to celebrate as a family.

53

The heat of the day was leaving, making the air much more comfortable. Dahameen sat on a small stool outside the slave quarters and thought over the events of the last hour. Remembering his own father who was also a slave in the household of Naaman's father, he understood the familial ties of knowing what happens when a family is reunited from being broken apart.

Dahameen's grandfather was a captive slave by Naaman's father, who was a captain in the Syrian army. His own father was just a babe of three or four at his capture, and at the age of 19, his father married one of the maidservants who served the captain's wife. Within a year, he was born, then a baby sister, and lastly, Amram.

His sister was sickly at birth and died from a disease when she was very young. The illness was brought about by a plague that had overtaken the city and her little body was too weak to fight the illness.

Dahameen's grandfather had ingrained the Hebrew faith into his son, who passed on that knowledge to him. His family was of the tribe of Levi and he was taught the rites of a priest. His father and mother were well taken care of and lived a good life until they passed on. His family was treated well under the old captain and when Naaman was young, Dahameen was chosen as the servant who would attend him. The only commandment Naaman's father had expressly given Dahameen was to not discuss anything about the Hebrew slaves' God, for only he and his wife would give religious instruction to their son, for the Syrians worshipped Rimmon and other minor gods.

Yet, young Naaman was not stupid and, as a child, would constantly question him and other slaves about the God they worshipped. How could the Israelites worship something they could not see? Their God had no form.

Having no personal knowledge of Yahweh, Naaman eventually stopped questioning and as he grew older followed the gods of the Syrians.

Dahameen's brother, Amram, would sometimes tell young Naaman about Yahweh, but remembering the old Captain's instructions, would not go into a deep explanation.

Now, Naaman and his wife asked many questions about Yahweh: His providence, His miracles, the Prophet Elisha, and Hebrew history. Since his healing, Naaman and Tirah asked a lot of questions and now Dahameen and Amram were only too happy to explain and discuss.

His mind went back to Naaman's betrothal and marriage. A year or two after his marriage to Tirah, first a rash, then the leprous boils began to show on his arms and body. By this time, Naaman had risen to the rank of Commander. Even though their marriage was an arranged one, he and his wife loved each other very much.

Tirah was raised vastly different from most Syrian women. When she came to Naaman, even he realized she was a woman of great compassion and knowledge. Unlike other women, she could read and write. Although she worshipped Rimmon, she knew of the many gods worshipped by the slaves in the compound. She also believed in fairness and treating others as she would herself.

When Naaman suggested to her that he would move into another building so she would not be infected, Tirah refused. She wanted to always be near him even if they could not fully live as husband and wife. It was then that Naaman requested Dahameen and Amram to personally serve him and protect his wife. He could have forced them to do so for they were his slaves, but Naaman realized that one cannot force someone to do a good job or be loyal.

He was afraid they would refuse because of the Israelite religious laws concerning leprosy, but they did not. He knew the Israelites followed the Mosaic laws and kept their lepers outside of the city or town. Naaman was not sure of the loyalty of all of his soldiers, but he was very sure of the loyalty of Dahameen and Amram and their families. He also knew Tirah felt the same about Sunih and her family.

Dahameen stood as two carriers came around the corner of the house. Lowering their burdens, the bearers stood tall before him. Commander Naaman stepped from one carrier and reached into the other to help Mistress Tirah out of hers.

"All is well, Dahameen?" It was more of a statement than a question. Bowing low and smiling, he answered, "Yes, my lord, all is well." The couple was then met by General Meruru and Mistress Petra and the four proceeded into the house.

Amram came into the healing room and announced that a small meal would be served in another room of the house. He led the family of Elah down the hall to a small curtained room with a large table. As they settled themselves, the curtain was pushed aside and servants entered with bowls and platters in their hand and began to serve the meal.

Aleea and Pua walked into the room carrying food in the same bowls that Sheera had delivered. Sheera clapped her hands as they smiled at her. Behind them Sunih carried a small carafe of wine, and a smaller girl entered to place another bowl with dates, nuts and pomegranates.

Sheera and Obid gave a joyous cry as they looked at the little one. "Pridi!" As Pridi came toward them, Elah gave a shout and Obid and Amir ran to her. Sheera grabbed her and gave her a kiss. More hugging and more crying took place. Sheera hugged Aleea and Pua and behind them came Shatii with a water jug. Introductions were made as Amram informed them that he had an assignment in General Meruru's house and would return later.

After awhile, Sunih gave a silent signal and Pua, Aleea and Pridi returned to the kitchens.

After they finished eating, Sheera began clearing the table as her family conversed. She wondered if she should take the used eating utensils to the kitchen, but was not sure of its location for she had never been inside the General's kitchen.

At that moment a tall male slave entered and began stacking with her. Obid and the slave stared at each other. Even though he was wearing the slave band of General Meruru's household on his arm, Obid knew his former adversary and later friend, Ewslet.

"Ewslet? You are no longer a mine slave?" After a slapping and hugging greeting, Ewslet smiled at him and explained, "That greedy pig, Shobach, told the Legionnaire that we were related in order to get more money. I guess he told General Meruru we might be related because we worked together. After all, we're both Israelites! That money-grubber knew we were from different Samaritan villages, yet he said he felt we should stay together. So I guess we'll have to continue our argument outside of the mines."

Obid clapped him on the shoulder and introduced Ewslet to his family.

On seeing Sheera, Ewslet laughed as he admitted, "You were truthful, Obid; your sister really is beautiful!" Sheera blushed and Ewslet and Obid laughed as once again they hugged each other. Ewslet finished stacking the pottery and took his leave.

Conversation continued and out of respect, no one said anything to Elah, for he had turned his face to the wall and was silently sobbing.

54

"Good morning, Jesse. Is there a reason you're visiting me this early in the day? Or is it because you came to see someone in particular?" Sunih smiled at her grandson who cast his eyes downward and blushed.

Her grandson was a good-looking slave, bronzed and muscular. She had noticed Jesse arriving early three or four days each week for the past couple of months. Sometimes he came to her quarters to talk abut nothing in particular, but would stand near the main door in order to catch a glimpse of Sheera as she went about her morning chores.

It was nothing new, for she had also noticed Sheera making herself visible so she could cast her eyes on Jesse. They would make a silent excuse to stand and talk in the long hall and each would ask about the other's day or discuss their duties. Sunih was not adverse to their strange courtship, but did not want either to skip their chores or get into trouble. General Meruru's wife was very kind to Jesse and the Mistress adored Sheera, but she wanted them to be aware that they were still servants — officially slaves — in their respective households and could easily be whipped, sold or killed if they were not in their rightful places when called.

As she walked to the Commander's rooms to remove the Master and Mistress' eating utensils following breakfast, she peered into the kitchen area and saw Amir and Pridi in a corner talking with their heads together. Not a problem she thought, perhaps because of their youth, but it seemed as if children were growing older every day.

55

One morning, while clearing the dishes from the Commander's table Sunih turned to see Mistress Tirah walking back into the room with worry shown on her face. In fact, it seemed as if she had been crying. Tirah asked Sunih to sit because she wanted to discuss something with her. The Commander had already left and they were alone. She led Sunih over to the long couch and both sat facing each other. Sunih waited for the Mistress to collect herself before she began speaking.

"Sunih," began the Mistress quietly, "has any of my maids said anything about wanting to be betrothed or married, or have they set their eyes on any of the soldiers or male servants that you are aware of?" Sunih stopped working and looked askance at her. The Mistress slowly continued. "Many of my husband's generals have soldiers who have observed my maids in town as well as when they are here in the compound. It seems they are looking for wives and I know my maids are of a marriageable age, but I don't want to lose them."

"Aweh has a man in her sights who is a member of Naaman's loyal servants and my husband has already given her in betrothal. She will become wife to Azariah in a few years and they are willing to wait because of her betrothed's schedule, commitment and travels with my husband. When they marry, she will continue to be near me and will continue in her duties, so I'm not worried for her."

"Some of the soldiers have more than one wife, and I am not in agreement with that. When Naaman and I married, we agreed one wife, one husband."

At this point, the Mistress' voice trembled. "They are my maids, but they really belong to my husband and this is the second time he has broached the subject of them perhaps wishing to marry. I believe it is because the men are anxious for they have not been in any battles lately and have been home for some time now. I know many want sons to carry on the family line, but I don't know many of the soldiers well enough to know how my maids will be treated.

"I so want to see my maids happy, but I am also selfish for I do not want changes. I want to be happy also." She stopped on a sob. "I'm sorry Sunih. Since this pregnancy, it seems I cry all the time for the silliest things. And I have more than a month to go. Please forgive me."

Sunih smiled and patted her shoulder. "I have an idea, Mistress. Do not worry so, for you do not want to distress your pregnancy. Give me a week." At this Tirah looked relieved and Sunih began formulating a plan.

Tirah remembered when she first married the Commander, he had not risen up the ranks at that time. He brought Sunih and her late husband into the marriage and made her his wife's personal slave. Over time the two women became friends and later confidants.

When Sunih's daughter and her husband died of the plague, Sunih brought their children, her grandchildren, to the Mistress. Leda became one of her personal maids, and her grandson, Jesse, was soon placed into General Meruru's household by the Commander.

With the Commander's leprous condition, it seemed no children would be born from their union so Leda soon became the Mistress' maid and filled the void as her daughter. The child was young, but she learned quickly and even though sickly, she did the best she could.

After Leda's death, the Mistress mourned her as if she was her child. When she purchased Sheera, Pua and Shatii, her heart began to heal. And now, if those maids were given away in marriage or betrothal, the Mistress would miss them for they were her constant companions -- especially Sheera.

She knew if she put her problems into Sunih's hands, things would work out all right. Right away Tirah began to feel much better and waddled away in search of the comfort food that Sunih always placed in her sleeping quarters each day.

It seemed she craved some of the strangest food lately, but Sunih made sure that whatever she had a taste for was at her disposal.

56

Sheera was cleaning in the back area, even though it was not in need of any maid work. Sunih approached her and put her arm around her waist while leading her to the end of the long hall. The younger woman looked questioningly at the elder as she was led to a stool. Sunih pulled another stool close by and began to speak quietly to her.

"Sheera," Sunih began, "even though you are in the Commander's compound and have many freedoms, I hope you understand that you are still a slave." Sheera nodded and waited. "You and the other girls are of a marriageable age and many of the Commander's men as well as his generals' soldiers have been requesting brides. There is no war going on and they are home now, so they want wives. They have seen all of you and know you are all fair to look upon. The Mistress wants you to marry, but as females you would have to go live with your husbands. The Mistress does not want to lose you or the other maids through marriage.

Sheera's eyes grew large as she began to understand Sunih. She knew other slaves did not have the freedoms that she, Shatii and Pua enjoyed. Some of the female slaves had been given in marriage to Syrian and other men they did not know or love, or many of them were in abusive marriages. Slaves were bartered and sold to the soldiers for marriage and some of them became the second and third wives in a household. Oftentimes they became concubines or mistresses to their Masters and then given away if a new concubine was added to the household. If the men's Masters were abusive, then such men would sometimes exhibit the same abusive tactics over their wives. Wives, like slaves, were the men's property.

Israelite marriages were vastly different than Syrian marriages. She and the other maids had been in Damascus long enough to be aware of these things and would sometimes discuss it among themselves, praising Yahweh that they were with the Mistress and not in another household. She began to worry that this might change. Her parents' marriage was one of love and devotion to each other and that is what she wanted. She lifted her eyes to Sunih with fear in her face.

Sunih continued. "If any of the Commander's men, or even General Meruru's soldiers or servants strike you as someone to whom you'd rather be betrothed, then perhaps that man could be considered. The Master would not just give you to anyone, but to satisfy his wife, he would look at General Meruru's men as well as his own first in order to keep you in the vicinity. I will also be discussing this with Shatii and Pua today, but I want you to know that the Mistress loves you girls and would want you here or close by."

Hope showed in Sheera's face as Sunih watched and thought, now to talk to the other girls. As she turned to leave, Sheera lightly touched her arm.

"Sunih," she started, and then lowered her eyes.

"Yes?" the older woman replied, waiting.

"Do you think your grandson, Jesse, ... I mean ... has he ever asked about me? I know he's here a lot making deliveries, bringing messages to the Master from General Meruru, or sometimes even comes to visit you ...". Her voice slowly dwindled away as her face became suffused with color.

At that moment, Sheera heard the Mistress calling her name. She turned and looked at Sunih and then ran toward the front without waiting for Sunih's response.

Sunih gave a chuckle and hurried in search of Pua and Shatii. She was also aware that those two maids had eyes on two of the carriers at General Meruru's compound, but she was not sure which two since Meruru had at least eight to ten male slaves who rotated the work. Then, too, there were soldiers who stayed around after delivering messages, so there was always the chance that one of them might be a choice of the girls. Who knew?

That night, the three maids discussed what Sunih had informed them. "Why now? Why can't those men just leave us alone and let us make our own decisions?"

"First of all, we are slaves. We can never forget that! But most probably because they need a wife for cooking, cleaning and fulfilling their physical needs." Pua was not sure those reasons were all bad, but wanted a choice in which man she wanted to give herself to.

Shatii expressed her willingness to marry, but said she also wanted to choose her own man and the others agreed. It was at this point that the three maids discussed who they hoped might want to ask for each of them.

All agreed they were happy that Sunih gave them advance warning. They knew the Commander would listen to his wife — wouldn't he? They also conceded that even though the Mistress would have input, she, too, was a woman as well as the Commander's wife. She was his property, even though he did not treat her as such.

At this, the three girls began to pray over the situation, asking Yahweh to intervene in their favor. None of the three slept very well when they finally went to bed.

57

Within the next two days, Obid, Jesse and Ewslet came one by one to the Commander's head servants requesting an audience with Commander Naaman and General Meruru.

Dahameen and Amram later reported to Naaman's quarters with great smiles on their faces. As they approached and bowed low, Naaman rose from his seat and told them to pull up seats and all three sat.

"Well," started the Commander, "did the plan work? Sunih predicted six to seven days, but it is only – what? – three days? What happened?"

Amram started to chuckle. "I had earlier spoken to them as if there was gossip circulating that offers were being made by the soldiers to marry your maids. I really thought Jesse was going to be ill; Obid rocked on his heels, and poor Ewslet looked so sad, I almost felt like putting my arms around him. Then they came later to see if you would discuss with them the chance to marry certain of the maids." He continued to chuckle a bit louder. Naaman and Dahameen joined in and soon they had full belly laughs.

Naaman wiped his eyes and said, "I told the plan to General Meruru and he is in complete agreement. Like Mistress Tirah, Mistress Petra is also worried. She has told the General she doesn't care who wants her maids; she will hide them first where no one will ever find them. She and Tirah seem to have a place that no one knows about except the two of them. And their carrier bearers will never tell because they are very loyal to their mistresses."

Petra and Tirah were great friends for they had grown up together in the same area of Syria. They had found strange places to which they would disappear when they wanted to be alone to talk where no one could hear. The only ones who knew of their secret area were the bearers who take them there. All three men had a great laugh as Dahameen and Amram continued to discuss with the Commander what had transpired to date.

Dahameen smiled as he related, "Once I asked one of the Mistress' bearers where they took the women and he only shifted his eyes to look at the candle holder, then the walls and then the ceiling. I could see he was beginning to sweat and looked very nervous; he wouldn't look me in the face and would only tell me that they always took the women wherever they were told. I believe their mistresses have sworn them to secrecy so I did not want to distress him any further and left him alone. I could see the relief in his eyes when I quit questioning him."

Naaman smiled at this. "Since Petra and Tirah share secrets, you can be sure all the young maids will be well hidden, and you are certainly correct! The carriers are very, very loyal to their mistresses, almost as loyal as mine are to me."

"Now I want both of you to inform those three men that I will meet with them following the evening meal here in my quarters. I need to get Meruru here because Jesse and Ewslet belong to him while Obid belongs to me. Send a messenger to inform him of what has taken place. We'll need to talk to them one by one. We both need to sit in on these meetings."

"First we'll speak with Ewslet, then Obid, and lastly Jesse. I know the three of them are shaking with anxiety while you both are in here asking their permission to speak to me, so let's make this meeting last a long time. Let's let them worry a bit longer. Any other news you have for me? Eh?

The men talked for some time explaining the duties of the new slaves, city news, telling experiences among the servants, gossip that the servants had picked up whenever they were in the city and news from the foreign traders who pass through the city. When the three finished talking, all went to their separate businesses.

58

That evening Jesse and Obid sat outside Naaman's quarters anxiously waiting for Ewslet to come out of the meeting with the Commander and the General. Were they all whispering so no one could hear? It was too quiet in the hall and they could not hear a thing. To make sure they did not get too close to the doorway, Dahameen sat outside the room.

Both thought, how long was Ewslet going to stay in that room? Why was Ewslet first? He didn't even know if Aleea even had any feelings for him. He just wanted to put his request in to General Meruru before someone else offered for her. After all, Obid thought, he had been with the Commander longer than Ewslet had been with General Meruru.

Jesse's thoughts were almost the same as Obid's. He had been with General Meruru longer than Ewslet and besides, he was the elder of the three and would sometimes work alongside the Commander's men as well as the General's. Why were they ahead of him? He already had the permission of Sheera's father.

Elah was elated! He knew before he asked to court his daughter that Elah would say yes! Not just because he had nursed him back to health, but also because Elah treated him like a son. Elah also knew Sheera had taken a fancy to him, but felt as slaves, it was best that Jesse speak with the General and the Commander for their permission to court or become betrothed.

As slaves they really had no say-so as to whom they fell in love with. Many Masters did not allow their slaves to marry the one they had feelings for. Sometimes the male was sold if he seemed to put his eyes on a certain female slave or the female slave was sometimes given to someone else. Few Masters would permit liaisons among their slaves in order to avoid the problems that sometimes arose.

Neither Amram nor Dahameen had said anything to him or the others about such news, but then again, they had not asked.

Jesse began to think that it would have been better to speak to Mistress Petra or even Mistress Tirah. After all, both women liked him and Mistress Tirah was grateful for the care he gave to Sheera's father. He knew Mistress Petra and the General appreciate his work for he had been promoted to accompany the Commander and the General on their excursions and was now a personal servant. The General had since asked him to train Ewslet to his old position.

Sheera was beautiful and in his mind she belonged to him. Jesse had never discussed his feelings with her, but knew she felt the same. However, there was always an off-chance that the Commander might betroth her to someone else, one of his soldiers perhaps, but that had not been announced in the slave quarters. Gossip was rampant among the slaves for they observed or heard from others what was going on in the city, the palace or among their own Masters.

Jesse had traveled with General Meruru and the Commander not long ago and realized Sheera could have found someone in his absence. Or a betrothal of Sheera to an unnamed slave could have been given in his absence. Suddenly Jesse was very nervous and could feel his hands becoming sweaty. What would happen or what would be said in his meeting?

Ewslet came out of the meeting with a big smile on his face. He walked past Obid and Jesse without saying a word, but his eyes seemed to have tears in them. Obid and Jesse looked at each other, but did not say anything. At that moment, Amram came out and whispered something to Dahameen, who turned and called for Obid to enter the room.

Little did either young man know that Ewslet's request had been answered in the affirmative. He had been secretly courting Aleea whenever he could meet with her. The first time he saw her by Mistress Petra's quarters, he knew he loved her. She was so pretty and walked so feminine.

They had been discreet, and he was sure she loved him. He knew that he loved her and now he had permission to pay court.

59

The audience of men sat outside the main housing unit at the rear of the birthing tent. The air was electric, not so much by the loyal soldiers and servants waiting with Naaman for news of his wife, but by Naaman himself. The Commander was fraught with worry about his wife as well as impatient due to the lack of information from inside the tent.

Inside the tent, Sunih laughed along with the three midwives who were awaiting the birth of the Mistress and Commander's baby. Sunih, along with Sila, Bernat, and Ammina, all loyal servants and midwives who served in the Commander's household, took a great deal of care with this birth. For the birth of a child for the Commander and Mistress Tirah was long in coming and the household was ready for the laughter of children.

The women had been hand-picked by the Mistress when she realized she was pregnant. Having previously discussed her pregnancy with Sunih, she began making plans for her child's birth, selecting male servants for the fixing of the nursery, making decisions concerning the types of material for the infant's clothing, and other matters for her baby's impending birth.

As soon as the pregnancy had been announced, Sheera, Pua and Shatii quickly went to work in the spinning room making beautiful sets of clothing for the newborn. Now proficient with wool and other materials, Risa worked with wool from newly sheared sheep to produce small blankets and other coverings. She brought her knowledge of dyes and made them different colors. They sang as they worked and the other servants smiled when they would hear them.

Her most beloved servants had made the Mistress comfortable, harking to her every need. When she craved certain foods, they were supplied. At this time, there was a great amount of anticipation as everyone awaited the birth of the Master and Mistress' child.

The Mistress tried to laugh at their jokes but was having strong labor pains. "Oh, Sunih, there must be a million babies inside of me," she panted. "I have never felt such pain! Oh, oh, oooohhhhh!" She turned her head from side to side while squeezing Sunih's hand. Feeling a responding squeeze, she was assured of Sunih's constant presence.

"I pray you will have a few fingers left when this is over. Oh, oh, please stay with me," she panted. "Don't leave me!!! Ooohhh! Why is this called a birthing stool? It should be called a torture stool! Please let this child come out!"

Her friend, Petra, had sat with her for some time during the beginning of her labor pains. When her water broke, Petra was visiting with her friend. Petra had calmed her and called for Sunih, who quickly felt it was best for Petra to go home. Petra was a few months pregnant herself and Sunih did not feel she should stay around her Mistress at this time.

"Let me know when I can come back." Petra wanted to leave Aleea with Sunih in case she needed the extra maid, but Sunih advised her and Aleea to leave. When all was completed, she and her household would be notified. Petra understood and she and Aleea soon took their leave from the birthing tent.

Petra herself was only in her fifth month of pregnancy and General Meruru was very happy. "Don't you find it to be strange that Petra and Tirah do almost everything pretty much around the same time?" he had jokingly remarked to the Commander.

Bernat was sitting on the floor rubbing the Mistress' legs to help with circulation. Tirah was in so much pain that she did not feel the hand of the midwife who felt inside her womb. Bernat nodded her head as she looked at Sunih and then held up two fingers, at which all of the women began to smile at each other. Ammina reached for more swaddling cloths as Sila dipped a piece of coarse cloth in the cool water and began wiping the Mistress' perspiring brow. Ammina leaned forward and whispered, "Soon, my lady, very soon. Your baby is ready to enter the world. Now push and push hard," she commanded.

"I can't – I hurt — I'm too tired! Unnnhhh!" she grunted. "It's been hours and hours," she moaned as she bore down as instructed. Bernat smiled and once again held up her hand with the index finger showing so that the others could see and all thought here comes the baby! "Aha, here's what we've been waiting for." The infant came out quickly and soon a whimpering cry burst forth from the blood-soaked baby and the women began clapping when Ammina announced, "He's a male child!"

The Mistress began to cry. "A blessed male child!" she sobbed. "Naaman will be so … Ahhhhh! What is happening?" Tirah panted as another contraction interrupted her comment.

"Bear down, my lady, bear down and push again," Bernat cried. "Ammina, more warm water for the other has decided to come now."

The Mistress stopped panting and looked surprised. "Other? What other? Unnhhh!" Eventually, another baby worked its way out and a sharp cry was heard as it took its first breath.

"Look my lady, this one is a girl and is as pretty as your son is handsome." The tent full of women began to laugh and cry in unison as they celebrated the birth of twins. Then the servants all laughed at the look of surprise on the face of their Mistress.

Sunih helped her rise from the birthing stool and cleaned her using herb water, oils and perfume, and changed her gown. Soon Tirah was laid down on the thick mat that had been prepared by Sunih and the other midwives earlier, while Bernat began cleaning the area around the birthing stool. The leftover cord was thrown into the fire.

Tirah watched as Ammina and Sila wiped the babies clean of blood with warm herb water and olive oil as both infants cried lustily. After they were wrapped in clean linen, the women laid the babies on each side of her chest, situating the babies to make sure she would not roll on top of them. Soon after, both babies slowly closed their eyes and slept the sleep of tired newborns.

"They are so beautiful," Tirah softly breathed while looking from one to the other; "so beautiful," she murmured and promptly fell into restful slumber.

Together the four servants finished cleaning up, removing the stool, lighting fragrant candles and putting fresh straw on the floor of the tent. They added more small branches to the brazier to keep the area warm, then silently left the tent.

60

"How long? How long?" Naaman paced the room. "Why won't they let me in there? After all, I am the Master of this place! I should be able to go anywhere I please!" He slammed his right fist into his left hand as he angrily kicked at the dirt.

Dahameen looked pityingly at him and patted the seat. "Commander, please sit. We may all be here for many more hours. Babies come when Yahweh wishes and undoubtedly He does not wish for the birth to take place at this time."

Amram and Ab-Hiren sat calmly at the table. A few soldiers waited outside the Commander's house playing a game of hands, which was similar to the throwing of lots. All had been inside and outside the house and compound as they waited with the Commander for most of the day.

It was now evening and no news had come from the tent for many hours. Once, however, Sila pushed the curtains aside as she slowly walked toward them saying, "Soon, Master, very soon." Then she turned as she left him and slowly walked back, again pushing the curtains aside and re-entered the tent.

Three house servants came inside the room bringing bread, roasted meat, cheese, fruit, wine and fresh water. The soldiers stopped their game and began eating and talking quietly together.

The Commander walked outside and paced for another few minutes until one soldier said, "Sir, with my first child, my wife labored for three days. There really is nothing you can do but wait!"

The other men who had children began voicing their wives' labor times, mentioning eight hours, two days and four days, almost as if in competition, and he was amazed. Naaman looked at them in wonder.

Dahameen gave the soldiers a quelling look that silenced the men. "This is only your first, my lord. You'll be much more calm when the others come." The soldiers laughed when they saw the Commander's confused scowl.

Still showing amazement, Naaman mumbled, "I don't know if I'll survive this one. At least in battle, there are planned strategies, timetables, and meetings. You knew what to expect." He then sat by the door on a little stool too small for his large frame and put his head in his hands: shakily running his fingers through his hair. He noticed his soldiers and servants were grinning at each other, but they kept silent.

A thought occurred to him. "Have any of you ever been inside the birthing tent? What goes on in there?" The men were aghast, looked at him in horror, and began talking as one.

"Oh, no sir!" "It is better to die in battle than in that tent!" "The women will kill you." "You can't go in there!" "Men are not allowed until the baby comes." "I wouldn't try going in there!" "Not me!" "Me either!" "We'll follow you into battle, but not into THE TENT!" They began laughing at the idea.

Naaman was puzzled, but decided not to ask any more questions about going into the birthing tent. So much for that idea, he thought. Women have too many secrets. Even the birthing tent is a secret.

He thought back to when his wife first told him of her pregnancy. She had a certain glow about her that he had never noticed before. She sat next to him on the couch and took his hands in hers, placing them on her belly. She looked him in his eyes and said softly, "I am with child."

He was stunned! Since his healing he had often wondered if they would ever have any children. It was now over two years since he bathed in the Jordan on the advice of the Israelite Prophet. Would his children inherit his disease? He had many questions, but his loyal Israelite servants, Dahameen and Amram explained to him that Yahweh does not do things halfway. They assured him that if Yahweh gave him and his wife children, they were quite sure any he produced would be clear of the disease.

After a while he began to anticipate the birth of his child. Would his child be a son whom he could teach to ride a horse, throw a javelin or spear, or the other activities a young male son of a Commander, should learn. He would have the smiths to make a small set of armor for his son. But then, what if she's a girl? Would she look like his wife: have her beauty and poise, and possess a sweet demeanor? When she reached a certain age, would he check out any man that wanted to marry her or would she hand-pick him? He had laughed at himself. The baby was not here yet, and already he had plans.

He made sure Tirah was well taken care of, but he needn't have worried. Once the compound's servants and slaves found out about the Mistress' condition, they took good care of her, whether he was at home or away. She and Sunih chose the midwives, material was purchased for the small room beside the Master bedroom, her maids began producing small outfits for the infant's clothing, carpenters were given instructions on how to furnish the nursery, etc.

Tirah was well loved and there really was nothing he could do. She always made sure he knew what she planned for the baby and since he felt women knew best, he left everything to her.

Before she told him of the baby, the Commander could see that his wife was feeling very much better lately. At first he thought she was catching a cold because she would be ill first thing in the morning, but later she would eat a full breakfast. The last few days she seemed to be feeling much better and it seemed she had acquired a lot of energy.

The other day she wanted to walk to visit her friend, Petra, but he put his foot down. When he said a few of his soldiers and her special servants would have to accompany her during the walk, she pouted for a few seconds, but saw the reasoning behind his suggestion. Later in the afternoon she did go visit Petra in her carrier with her bearers and four of her maids to walk beside it.

While Tirah visited with her friend, the maids were allowed to visit with Petra's maids and the bearers went to the back section of General Meruru's compound to visit with friends and the sick slaves in the healing rooms to await a call to take her back home.

Earlier in the year, a wife of one of the generals was almost abducted, but her bearers fought off the perpetrators and held them until the soldiers arrived. Of course, the three men were never seen again after the Legionnaires came to take them away. It was the intent of the perpetrators to hold the woman for ransom, but they were not aware that the general's wife's loyal servants were given the same training as her husband's soldiers. The two were badly outnumbered for the woman's servants fought like soldiers, easily overpowering them.

The news of the ambush was the topic of conversation not only among the slaves, but also among the wives and families of the soldiers. Following the aborted abduction, more servants and soldiers were required to accompany their families.

Naaman was well aware of the dangers of women traveling alone, as well as wives of the nobility. Damascus was like any other big city and crime was always prevalent.

61

A baby's faint cry from the tent interrupted his thoughts.

A baby! His baby was born! Naaman and his men began jumping up and down with joy! It reminded him once again of his joy at the Jordan River when his leprosy was cleansed. These were the same servants and soldiers who celebrated with him at the Jordan.

It was not long before they heard two separate infant cries. The men looked questioningly at each other and then at the Commander. At that moment, Naaman watched as Sunih slowly came out of the tent and headed straight toward him. He quickly rose from his seat and walked toward her.

"Sunih? Is my lady all right?" She gave him a huge grin, bowed before him, and slowly said, "Commander, your lady, your son and your daughter are all very well."

Sunih stood still and waited until the message sank in. Slowly it registered in the Commander's mind the two infant cries and what she had just said.

"A son and a daughter? Two?? I have two??" Once again, she said, "Your son and your daughter, as well as my lady, are all very well, my lord!" With that, she turned and slowly headed back toward the tent.

Naaman held up his hands and bellowed to his men, "I have a son AND a daughter!! I have two!" He ran after Sunih and hugged her, picked her up and swung her around. "I have two, Sunih, I have two!!"

"Yes," she quietly answered. "I know."

Naaman put her down, kissed her on both cheeks and allowed her to walk back to the tent. Sunih smiled her sweet smile and re-entered the birthing tent.

* * *

Signals were then given by the Legionnaires. A few minutes later a horn blew in the distance announcing to the compound and the surrounding area that the Commander's wife had given birth. Runners were soon dispatched with the news that the Commander was the proud father of a boy and a girl.

In the palace, King Ben-Hadad smiled as a messenger relayed the news to him. His great Commander was now a cleansed man, a proud husband and a new father.

The four midwives came out of the birthing tent a bit later and walked toward the compound. The Commander was told he could see his wife, but she would probably not know he was there for she was very tired and may continue to sleep.

Naaman pushed the tent's covering aside and headed toward the sleeping area where his wife lay with two small bundles, one on each side of her. Even though the lighting was very dim, he saw the two sleeping little ones.

Sunih moved the lamp stand a bit closer so he could see his new babies. As he watched, one of the bundles opened its little eyes and stared at him. Slowly the babe smiled, closed its eyes, and went back to sleep. Tirah turned her head and looked at her babies, then looked up at her husband's face. She could see he was pleased and smiled at him. She then gave a small sigh and returned to her slumber. Sunih touched Naaman lightly on the arm and signaled for him to follow her out of the tent.

As the sun set that evening, slave and free celebrated together the births of the infants. The Commander and his servants gave praise to Yahweh for their safe delivery. He would be allowed to see his wife and babies again on the morrow knowing Tirah would need her rest tonight to regain her strength. Sunih sent Amram to guide the exhausted Commander back to the house for she knew he needed the rest as well as his wife.

That night as he sat on the edge of his bed, Naaman bowed his head and gave a silent prayer of thanks to the unseen God for allowing his wife to make it through the ordeal and for giving him two children at once. He also gave thanks to the absent Prophet Elisha, whose prayers to the unseen God had made all things possible.

Giving a satisfied sigh Naaman finally fell into a pleasant asleep.

EPILOGUE

It was now three years later for Elah since he had been a slave in Commander Naaman's compound. This evening, as he sat under the nearby olive tree, he thought over everything that had happened within the last decade. He still became sad when he thought of the raid on his village, the loss of life and his family, and his ill treatment in the Syrian mines. But the last few years had been good.

When the head gardener became too old to work the fields, Elah was given the job as new head gardener over the fruits and vegetables grown on the properties of Commander Naaman and his wife. He was put over a group of slaves who worked with him in planting, harvesting, and storing the crops from the various fields.

Elah also had a small garden behind the house which supplied fruits and vegetables for the immediate slaves' homes. And the Lord had blessed him with fruitful harvests for these few years. Other slaves from households in the area would come to consult with him for planting and harvesting advice for their own Masters' crops. He worked well with General Meruru's gardener and had made many friends in the meantime.

In his village in Aphek, he was known to have the sweetest melons, flourishing wheat, glorious olive trees, and other fruits and vegetables. He showed other gardeners how the wheat should be separated in order to reap a larger harvest and how to separate the tares without pulling up all the good crops. Even Obid had redesigned some of the Syrian tools to resemble his tools from home to make the planting easier.

Elah had a smile on his face as he contemplated his life in front of the large slave house that had been given to Sheera and her husband by the Commander and Tirah as a wedding present. Sheera had moved her entire family into the house, which contained areas broken into sections, so that Elah and each of his children could reside near her. Of course, the family was still considered captive slaves, but in his heart he felt life was good.

The family was allowed to worship Yahweh according to the Commandments and the Laws of Moses. Amram and Dahameen were performing the duties of priests for the city's slave community in a small house of worship built by Hebrew slaves in the fields on property owned by Naaman.

* * *

Elah had just returned from a celebration of marriage of one of Mistress Tirah's maids by the name of Aweh, to her new husband Azariah, who was one of the personal soldiers under Commander Naaman. She was beautiful in a dress his daughter, Sheera, had sewn for her. The wedding celebration was still taking place, and many soldiers and slaves who worked for the various generals under the Commander were in attendance. Commander Naaman, Tirah, General Meruru and his wife, Petra had also dropped in to add their blessings.

Many of the Commander's slaves were given this day off to attend the ceremony, but he was now tired and decided to come home and rest. Work would begin once again in the morning.

Jesse and Sheera had made him a grandfather of a beautiful baby boy who was called Little Elah, and Sunih was now a great-grandmother. Sheera was still a personal maid, but since she had gained a command of other languages, she now studied with Aweh in how to settle arguments among the slaves.

Mistress Tirah had produced a set of twins, delivered by Sunih and other slave midwives. They were healthy toddlers — a boy the parents named Naaman II, and sweet little Naeri, who looked just like her mother. Both were trying to walk, but were fast crawlers and had to be watched every minute for they tended to touch everything before putting it into their mouths.

Mistress Petra, General Meruru's wife, had produced a son, who was just trying to walk. Elah always smiled whenever he saw the child, for little Mahal-Kamala was the spitting image of his father. Maha, as he was called, played with the twins often because of the close relationship of their parents, who visited each other quite often.

Pridi and Amir had recently celebrated their betrothal and will wed in a few years. Ewslet began working as a carrier bearer in the household of General Meruru, where he has been betrothed to Aleea. Their wedding would be within the year.

Pua had taken over the position of personal maid, working alongside Sheera to Mistress Tirah, and will soon wed one of the head servants who had traveled to Samaria with the Commander. Shatii had been given the responsibility of Commander and Mistress Tirah's children as their nanny. She also had recently become betrothed to one of General Meruru's personal soldiers.

The Commander, General Meruru and their wives had laughingly agreed they were beginning to love betrothals and weddings because there was always a party held following such a ceremony. Both were pleased that it was within their joint households and neither would lose a servant or slave.

His son, Obid, was training with Dahameen to perform some of his same duties and was allowed to travel with the Commander on many of his journeys. The Commander treated Obid as one of his personal servants and he was very proud of this fact.

Elah believed that Obid and Risa would eventually marry as soon as the Commander gave them permission to do so. They had been betrothed for almost a year and everyone was in agreement with the courtship.

Upon hearing soft steps, he looked up and saw Sunih coming toward him. The older woman had a smile on her face as she appeared on the crooked trail to his house. As she came closer, he pulled up a small stool and helped her sit as he returned her smile. In her arms she held Little Elah.

When the baby saw his grandfather, he held his chubby arms out to him and Elah took him from Sunih. Within minutes of sitting on Elah's lap, the little one fell into a peaceful sleep. Both of them looked at the baby and then each other and smiled.

"Life is good, is it not Elah?" she asked. "Yes, Sunih," Elah replied. "Praise Yahweh. Life is good and all is well!"

ARUSHIL'S HANDS

ARUSHIL'S STORY IS TAKEN FROM
THE HOLY BIBLE, LUKE 17:11-17

NOTES ABOUT
ARUSHIL'S HANDS

The Bible gives an account of 10 lepers who had contracted the disease of leprosy. They were the "unclean," living on the outskirts of town. Lepers were disdained by the villagers and forced to roam the hills on the outskirts of villages and towns. This was in accordance with the Levitical Laws on cleanliness as well as the fact that no one wanted to "catch" the disease.

I named the main character "Arushil" and gave him a family and named a few of the nine other lepers who were his friends. Of course the story that follows is not written as true, although based upon scripture. It is my version of what took place following the main character's healing.

Nothing is revealed about this leper other than the fact that he, along with nine others, was cleansed of this dreaded disease. Upon being healed by Jesus, all 10 were told to go and show themselves to the priests. He was the only one to return to say thanks to Jesus for his healing.

During one of the adult Sunday School classes at my church, a question was asked "Why didn't Jesus allow the man to thank him and then send him on to catch up with the other nine as they headed toward town? After all he was healed along with the others." It was agreed that since his ethnic background was that of a Samaritan, he would still have been shunned by the Jews.

Scriptures relate how Jews and Samaritans generally did not mix, and as a Samaritan he would still be considered an outsider or non-Jew and, therefore, discriminated against. Historically, Samaritans were not considered pure Jews, but a mixed race which relocated to the Northern Kingdom of Israel after returning from the Assyrian and later Babylonian captivities.

I decided to let Arushil tell his story to his daughter-in-law in order to give the reader a bit more information on his condition and healing. Hopefully, my readers will enjoy this story and receive a bit more insight into the plight of a leper during Biblical times as well as understand Jesus' compassion on the "unclean."

ARUSHIL'S HANDS

1

Arushil slowly washed his hands in the basin of sudsy water, turning his hands this way and that, palms up then palms down. "Opah," his grandchildren called to him. "Opah, Opah!" the children called as they rushed into the room.

He smiled and responded, "I'm here, my loves. Come to me in the back room."

He did not move away from the wash basin. It never ceased to amaze him how perfectly formed his hands were or how his body seemed to slowly age over the years. He was still a fit man, never suffering headaches, muscle or joint pains or any physical illnesses as other men his age. Still handsome in his middle age, he had few facial wrinkles and his arms were as strong and muscular as an 18 year old. His beard had a few gray strands, but the hair on his head was glossy and black, with very little gray at his temples.

"What are you staring at, Opah?" "Is something on your fingers?" "What is it?" "Why are you staring at your hands?" As his grandchildren threw their questions toward him he only smiled, for they always had many questions but failed to wait for an answer. They continued on, their words interrupting each other. The baby girl climbed into his lap and patted his face as she smiled into his eyes and received her grandfather's kiss on her forehead.

"Omah said to hurry and come to the table for the food is ready!" "The meal is ready, Opah!" "Come and eat!" Their words tumbled over the other as each tried to tell the message first.

As they reached him, his wife followed behind the two small boys and baby girl into the room. She smiled as she told the children to let Opah finish washing and go to the table so they could have their midday meal. The two boys ran toward the front of the house with the baby girl waddling behind as she stood over her husband.

"Come Arushil, the midday meal is ready." Her husband patted the hands that rested on his shoulders after drying his face and hands. "I'm coming, my dear," he replied.

Uzza was still a beautiful woman and stood tall and stately. Arushil loved looking at his wife, for in his eyes, she was still a young vibrant girl. He realized he was a bit hungry and stood, allowing her to take his hand and lead him from the grape room to the main part of the house.

As Arushil and Uzza began to situate themselves around the table, his son and daughter-in-law had already seated themselves across from Arushil and were smiling at the scene. The love that flowed through the house was very satisfying to the entire family. Even the young ones could feel the loving atmosphere.

"Arushil," his wife said, "the children are too young to know about you and your hands and why you look at them with such pleasure. Now, my dear, sit down and give thanks for our food!"

She smiled at her husband as the family held hands and bowed their heads while her husband gave thanks for the food, his family and home. Then, when he came to the end of the prayer, he added a strange blessing.

Arushil had said prayers for the meal many times, but at the end of this one, he added, "… and may the teachings of our Lord and Savior, Jesus the Christ, spread according to His Word." His daughter-in-law looked up quickly at Arushil. She had always found that some of her father-in-law's prayers had strange connotations but did not want to ask too many questions of her husband's family.

No one said anything following the prayer, for Uzza, the children and her husband began to pass the plates and bowls with constant chatter. Her questioning look was not lost on Arushil, who only smiled as he held his hands out for the large bowls that were being passed around the table..

Jehosha, Arushil's daughter-in-law, looked at her husband and raised her eyebrows, but no one else seemed surprised at his words. Whenever they came to visit her husband's family, she felt as if there were secrets in their house that were very pleasant, but were not explained. As she picked up her eating utensils, her husband, Joram, smiled and held up his index finger. She knew this was a signal that all would be explained at a later date.

Conversation at the table ensued and the children chattered to their grandparents, for each wanted to tell them something that happened during their trip to their house. The baby began striking her spoon against the wooden table letting everyone know she had something to tell also. Mealtime was a pleasurable time.

2

Following the meal and after putting the baby on a pallet for her nap, the two women began clearing the table. Grabbing water pots and other vessels, they headed toward the well with the two boys running alongside them. They discussed the activities of the children, current events, as well as friends and relatives they both knew.

Other women were taking turns getting water from the well in the center of town, which was known as "Jacobs Well." Everyone in Samaria knew of this well for it was noted for its fresh, clear and sweet water. The chatter of the town's women was normal for this time of day. They were able to exchange greetings and gossip, relate news, ask about the health of family and friends, and have general conversation. Once their pots were filled, the conversation slowly died down as the crowd of women began to disperse by twos and threes.

When Uzza and Jehosha reached home and placed their water pots on the table, Jehosha put her hand on her mother-in-law's arm and the older woman turned to her with a smile.

"I know what you wish to ask, my daughter, but it would be best to discuss it with my husband. He would be very happy to tell you. He will not bring up the healing, but if you ask him, he would be pleased. He's been waiting to tell you, but he wanted to be sure you were ready to hear what he has to say.

Jehosha was surprised. "Healing? Was my father-in-law sick before I met Joram? I have never seen him ill. Was he dying?" She could only think of healthy, virile Arushil as he looked every time she, Joram and the children came to visit. They would often visit for a few weeks or so during late summer and since the birth of the children, they began staying for a longer period so the grandparents could enjoy them.

"No, my daughter," Uzza smilingly replied, "just ask him about the healing." Jehosha noticed that Uzza never said "his healing" but "the healing." Strange, she thought.

3

Jehosha's opportunity to see Arushil alone came a few days later. Her mother-in-law had taken the children with her to the river to wash clothes and Joram had gone with them. With rambunctious boys of 4 and 5 years of age, and an 18-month old daughter, he knew the children would be too energetic for his mother.

Her father-in-law had gone to the small shed in the vineyard behind the house known as the "grape room" and was preparing the grapes for making the winter wine. She decided to take the worn path from the back of the house to that area and help him with the wine-making. She found him in the corner wrapping the ripe grapes.

Jehosha picked up some of the fruit from a great tub and began wrapping them in the material prepared for them. As she did so, Arushil turned around and smiled. Finally, she stood and hesitantly pulled a small stool toward him.

"Father," she began, "I have a question to ask you concerning your health. Mother told me you had been ill and she mentions your healing but does not give me any information. She suggested I speak with you. Do you have a moment?" She kept her head down in respect, while her eyes looked up, searching his face.

Arushil gave a slow smile and suggested she bring the small stool near the door to the room. As she sat, he drew another stool and sat facing her. She looked around the small room where he always fixed the grapes for wine and juice.

On the wall were large stirring sticks for the wine, two large vats, as well as two beautiful lyres and other stringed instruments. She was not surprised to see them for she knew that her father-in law would sometimes play the lyre in late evenings. his music always seemed to soothed. Had he once been so ill that he was unable to play his beloved instruments? She hoped that was not the case.

Arushil smiled at her as he stated, "My dear, it will take more than a moment to tell you about my healing, but I will always have time for you." Arushil folded his hands in his lap, looked up at the ceiling and then began his story.

"I see you are looking at my musical instruments. Beautiful aren't they? They were handed down from my grandfather and my father to me. They are all I have of my family since I have not seen them since I was very young. I was taught to play the lyre when I was young and even though I was not lonely, I sometimes kept to myself.

When I had nothing to do, I would pick up one of my instruments and play it. Then things started happening to my body and I had to stop." Jehosha stared at him and then at the instruments on the wall.

4

"I was about 15 when I broke out in a few small sores that were not very noticeable, so I didn't think anything of them. They began appearing on my hands and my torso. My parents were about to announce my betrothal to a childhood friend. She and I had been playmates since birth and it was natural that our families would merge for both families were vinedressers."

"There was a contract being made ready and the celebration date was set. It was agreed that I would play my instruments at the betrothal party and I began to practice day and night because I didn't want to make any mistakes. But my fingers would make sharp tinglings when I tried to strum the strings. Eliadah and I were both happy, but a few weeks before the celebration, more sores began to show over my hands, face and more of my torso. When we went to the synagogue, one of the priests checked my body and declared that they were leprous sores."

"Over a short time, the sores spread and began turning white. My betrothal contract was declared broken by Eliadah's father when the disease became known, and later Eliadah was betrothed to someone else."

"I was devastated – not because of the broken betrothal for we were not in love and had accepted it because that is the way of our people. It was because later the priests declared that I had to be placed outside the town."

Arushil put his head down and looked at his hands. He turned them palm side up and looked at her. "For three years I roamed the hill area on the outskirts of town, at first alone, but later aligning myself with other lepers. During that time Eliadah married and I heard she had produced two boys."

"My sores were slowly turning white and eating away at my skin, and I was upset that soon I might begin losing my ears and fingers. I think what worried me the most was the fact that I knew the fingers would shrivel and then fall off. I have always taken great pride in my hands. I have long fingers and as a youth I loved to play the lyre, but with the spread of the disease, I could no longer do so. I did not know how soon the various stages of the disease would take place. I was angry and afraid."

Jehosha's eyes were as big as saucers. She stared at Arushil and even behind his beard she could not see any leprous conditions on his smooth face and hands. "How can this be?" She had seen lepers before, but Arushil did not have any of the sores or white spots that were always present.

"Ah, I see you are thinking that I do not have such sores now, but I once did." Arushil chuckled at her observation of him. He pulled his stool closer to her and continued.

"In the meanwhile, there was a Man by the name of Jesus of Nazareth, a man of God who had the gift of healing. I was with nine other lepers in the hills and we had listened to traders and others who passed through the area near our caves telling how this Man could heal. He had been known to heal the sick and lame, but we wondered if he could heal lepers."

"Hope for us was almost gone, but he had been in the area a few times and more people would talk about Him and His teachings and we began to hear more of His healings. It was well known that whoever came to Him for healing was healed. There were times we would follow behind some of the traders and travelers when we heard He was nearby just to learn more about Him."

"We were able to hear him teach from afar because we were not allowed to be close to those who were not leprous. In fact, if we were within 10 feet of people, we had to yell "unclean, unclean" so others would know we were nearby. We weren't even allowed near the Temple, let alone inside the city. So any hope we had of meeting Jesus was naught."

"We were always praying for healing, but had begun to believe nothing would change and all ten of us began to give up hope. We also knew that over time we would all be dead or dying soon. The disease was spreading very quickly. All of us were at different stages of the disease and prayed every day for Yahweh to heal us, but nothing ever came of our prayers. Even though some of us were from other areas, except for myself, they were all Jews."

"Yet because of our disease, there was no distinction between us – religious differences or otherwise. For we were all lepers who are the most hated of humans. If we did not stick together, we would surely die a lonely death. The townspeople called us 'the colony'. And we were not the only colony for there were other lepers besides ourselves. Roaming lepers would eventually form their own colonies. We later realized that Yahweh put the ten of us together for His own purpose."

"Many people do not understand the plight of lepers. Some slowly die without friends or family. All they have are other lepers to live with. There are thefts of food among the lepers, for not all are able to receive food. We basically lived off the land, but on the outskirts of villages and in the hills. We also stole vegetables and food from orchards and trees. Sometimes we would catch a small animal, but it is very hard to cook when you're not sure one of your fingers or other body parts would fall into the fire."

"Our area was a dry desert and few plants grew there. We hunted the smaller animals for meat while we had strength. Those animals became scarce when the villages or towns began to grow and men moved their families to the outskirts, which meant we had to move also."

"As the towns and villages grew, they tended to move to where we were hiding and then we had to move also, for lepers have to stay on the outside of the towns or in the deserts and in caves in the hills."

"Then there are the animals which smell rotting flesh, especially carrion birds and scavenging animals and the insects who try to feed off of our sores. Some lepers are attacked by animals and eaten, which is one of the reasons it was best to get into a group, for there is safety in numbers."

"We were only ten, but knew there were other colonies of three to four, and even some with 15 or more. We had heard tales of lepers trying to settle into caves in which wild animals were already using. Our group made spears and stored big rocks in the event something of that sort happened, but praise Yahweh, we never had to use them."

"We couldn't beg in town for we were the unclean. Besides, no one would come near us to contribute alms. If we were able to have money, what merchant would sell us food? There was no way the people would accept money from our hands. Most people want lepers to stay on the outskirts in caves and hills or die so they won't have to be bothered with us. Being a leper is a painful and lonely life, my dear. The sores are one thing, but as it progresses, the pain becomes unbearable. Eventually there is no pain and one never knows when a body part will be missing."

Jehosha could feel her eyes tearing, but turned her head so her father-in-law would not see the moisture in her eyes or her pity as he continued.

Arushil had his back to her as he continued to relate his story. "In the beginning, when I first contracted the disease, my family would put food on the edge of town near the cave so I would not starve, and a few others had family members who would drop off bread, cheese, fruits and vegetables. Since we roamed the hills, it might be days before we returned to our regular hiding place."

"When I didn't show up for some time to collect my food, I was told my family believed I must have died. Eventually, my family moved away and then there was no more."

"Sometimes food is laid out for us, but if we did not get to the food quickly enough other lepers would run to steal it. We soon stayed in the areas so that when food was placed, we would be the first to get to it. Our colony made a practice of not trying to steal another colony's food if we saw it placed near our area. Not all colonies were honest, for receiving food was necessary to our livelihood."

5

"One of the leprous men in our group, Hezron, had a sister named Uzza, who would bring a good amount of food for him and we would share our meals together. We were the blessed ones for there were still loved ones who cared. We traveled the hills, but always came back to the same hill when we knew Uzza would be coming to visit with us."

"While eating she would be on one part of a hill and we would be on another. She called our hill "Lepers Hill." Her family was not happy about her visits, but Uzza had an independent spirit and loved her brother. She kept us informed of what was happening in the city, in our families and in the synagogue. She would sing to us and even taught us songs she learned from the priests."

"Uzza would even pray with us when we were discouraged. We always felt her prayers could reach Yahweh. We began calling her "Priestess Uzza" and we would have a small service on the hills as she related what happened during the services she attended in the synagogue. Uzza would listen to our complaints, but she always tried to lift our spirits.

He smiled at her when he saw her confusion. "Yes, she is my Uzza and I dearly love her. She is lovely to look at and has the most beautiful spirit. I know Yahweh sent her to me. I never loved Eliadah, but I dearly love my Uzza. She is my heart." Arushil's face took on a dreamy expression as he said this.

"One day, the ten of us were sitting on a low hill on the border between Samaria and Galilee and saw people from the village running toward us. It seemed Jesus of Nazareth was traveling toward Jerusalem. People were yelling and screaming, 'Jesus is coming! Jesus is coming!' So we ran on the outskirts of the people toward Him."

"Uzza had told us everything she'd heard about Him, His healings and His teachings, even though she herself had never actually seen Him. We didn't even know what He looked like, and although He was of average height and build, He had a certain presence about Him no one else had. While He and a dozen or so men were walking on the road toward us, we instinctively knew it was Him."

"He was traveling toward our village so we began shouting for him to heal us. 'Jesus,' we cried out and constantly repeated, 'have mercy on us!' We were ten voices strong as we walked and hobbled toward Him. We kept shouting as loud as we could to make ourselves heard. The crowd kept growing and making a lot of noise and we were afraid He might not even hear us, let alone see us."

"Ziljan, who was one of us, had almost lost his voice from the disease, for he had sores on his neck and inside his throat. But he continued shouting also. He was not able to swallow normally so he had lost a lot of weight. We headed toward the Healer and kept shouting, 'Jesus, have mercy! Have mercy upon us!'"

"And you know, He heard and saw us standing there together. He stopped walking and looked at us standing to the side of the crowd. The people did not come close to us, but stared at us with repulsion on their faces."

"The ten of us were trying to hold on to each other for our diseases were now approaching the latter stages. Hezron and I were holding up Ziljan for he was very weak and his limbs looked to be ready to fall off. Jeconiah's skin had started to peel on his fingers, feet, and toes. Soon they would be falling away for he had very little feeling in them. His greatest fear was that they would fall off and he would not know it. We knew he was worried about his smaller limbs – but we all continued heading toward Jesus shouting and pleading as one."

"And you know, Jesus the Healer stopped when He saw us standing there. He held his hand up to halt the people who were traveling alongside and behind Him. The village's people also stopped. Jesus did not look as if he was afraid of us or that we would contaminate Him as some of the townspeople were wont to do. He looked at all of us with the most compassionate eyes and I wanted to cry for there was no condemnation or pity. Even if Jesus chose not to heal us, just His concerned look was enough."

"But as He came toward us He spoke. In a low voice He said, 'All of you. Go into the village and show yourselves to the priests'."

"We were shocked at His words – for we couldn't go into the village! Show ourselves to the priests? They would yell at us to leave or throw rocks at us. But we turned on the road and did as we were told and as we headed toward the village, Jeconiah was the first to recognize his skin had changed."

"He looked at his fingers, which had been ready to fall off — and they were whole! Then he began to cry aloud, and when we looked at him, he held up both of his hands to let us see his fingers and hands. He lifted his right leg and we saw that his feet and toes were normal and clear. Then we all looked at ourselves." Arushil's eyes glistened as he thought of that moment.

"I turned and looked at Ziljan and saw he was walking on his own. His body no longer showed the white sores. We looked down at ourselves and saw that none of us showed any signs of the skin disease that had been with us for years. Even our clothes looked different."

"As we looked at each other we began crying, hugging, and praising the Lord. We danced and felt each others' hands and faces as we repeated, 'Yahweh is God! Yahweh is God!'!"

"The people knew us as the ten lepers. We were the colony which roamed outside the village; they knew who we were. Some heard us shouting and crying and came to see what our words were about. They were all amazed at the difference. They did not come toward us, but stared; even they could not believe we were the same lepers who lived on the outskirts. Although we had been made clean, I guess they were afraid to trust their eyes."

"As we continued walking toward the village, I saw that even my ragged clothes were now clean and intact. When I pointed this out to the others, they laughed and cried as we looked at one another. They also noticed their bodies and clothes were clean. The white was white and the brown was brown, and the green was green – not dusty, dirty and ragged. Jesus had healed us inside and out!"

6

Arushil face was exuberant! Jehosha could see that he was remembering that day as if it was actually yesterday and not years ago.

"We had not gone very far when I realized Jesus had asked nothing from us, not money or some type of favor. So I left my friends and turned back to thank the Healer. He did not have to heal me but He did! Praise the Lord! I was crying as I approached. He looked me in the face and I knew he could see that I was cleansed of that dreaded disease. I fell at His feet and began to worship Him."

"Thank you, Jesus, thank you! Glory to your name, oh Healer! You are truly the Son of the Living God! Yahweh be praised."

"I was crying and blubbering as I fell at His feet, but He didn't seem to care. I just could not stop crying. He was the first person I touched when I was healed and I was happy it was Jesus. My tears made the hem of His robe wet and I could feel his hands on my head as he smoothed back my hair for my hair, which was in patches, was now full. Jehosha, Jesus touched me! He touched me without any fear of catching my disease."

Jehosha was confused. "What about the others? Did they come back to thank the Healer?"

"Ah, Jehosha! They were so happy they were crying and leaping as they hurried on toward the village to reach the synagogue so they could show themselves to the priests. Their aim was to be declared whole as written by the laws of Moses."

"The Healer held out his hands to lift me to my feet as He asked my name. I told it to Him and said I was from a small village in Samaria. Then He asked about my friends. He did not seem surprised that the other nine did not come back, but the fact that only I, a Samaritan, returned to give Him praise. None of them came back at that time, but He noted although ten were cleansed, I was the only one who returned to say thank you."

"I have always believed the others would have done so, but they were so elated at their cleansing and intent on showing themselves to the priests that they must have forgotten. I don't know if they sought Him out later or not. I never asked them when I saw some of them much later. We were still celebrating our cleansing for years afterwards, although now I don't see most of them any more. But I knew – I knew I would never forget Who healed me."

The Healer never laid a hand on any of us or said a prayer over us, but He healed all of us with just His words. He healed me! I was a Samaritan and still am, but

He didn't take our backgrounds into consideration. He healed us regardless of the fact that all of us were unclean, diseased men!"

"Every day I praise Yahweh for sending such a Man to our area. I still think back on His surprise that out of the 10 of us, I was the only one to return to Him to thank Him."

"He asked me, 'Weren't there 10 lepers that were healed?' I still believe we were all so surprised at our healing that the others just forgot to thank him. As Jesus turned to leave, he turned back and said I should get up and go home."

"At the beginning I was ready to go toward the synagogue to show myself to the priests also, but He told me to go home. I was so joyous I almost forgot that as a Samaritan I would not be allowed in the Jewish temple. Once that fact became known, I would still be as a leper to the Jews. Without asking me, I believe Jesus knew this, but I was not offended. I was cleansed -- no longer a leper!"

7

"I returned to my cave in the hills to pick up what few belongings I had stored there and saw Uzza climbing up the hillside toward me. She had been looking for her brother. She did not recognize me and put her head down to adjust her scarf around her head as she began to pass me."

"As a young single girl, by Law she could not look me in the face. Otherwise she would be thought too forward. Whenever she came to visit us, she did not wear her scarf or shawl for it did not matter as there would be no physical contact between us."

"As I looked at her, I smiled. She gave a little smile back and when I greeted her by name, she looked up and gave me another slight smile, but I could see she did not recognize me for there were no boils or white areas on my skin — my face was clear and my clothes were clean."

"I again said, 'Good day, Uzza.' She still did not recognize my face but recognized my voice. 'Arushil,' she questioned while peering into my face. 'Is it you?' Then she was joyful. She looked as if she would come nearer, but stopped for she was not in the habit of being close to me — but I could see it in her eyes. I told her to have a seat on the hillside and there began to explain what happened to me, Hezron, Jeconiah, Ziljan, and the others."

At first she looked as if she did not believe her ears, then she began to cry. "'My brother, Arushil! What about Hezron? Was he healed also?' She continued crying as I told her the story of our healing and that she should be joyous for all ten of us She jumped up when I told her to go home for her brother will most likely return to the family home after visiting the priests."

"Uzza was somewhat puzzled. She asked, 'What about you, Arushil? Why did you not go to the village priests to be counted as clean?"

He smiled at the memory. "Uzza did not realize my background. You see, the other nine lepers were Jews, whereas I was a Samaritan and would not have been allowed inside a Jewish synagogue. In fact, Uzza would otherwise not have been able to talk to me, for not only was I one of the unclean, I was a Samaritan of what the Jews considered the 'mixed race.' And yet my family was pure. We had never married into other nations."

"That is why we live in this valley. We are the Samaritans that worship the same as the Jews – the villagers nearby consider us to be partially Sadducees, although I consider myself a Pharisee as well for I believe in the resurrection. Jesus was resurrected for He returned from the dead and was seen by many. And we follow The Way of Jesus the Christ!"

"In this area, we have a small synagogue, for we are not allowed in the Temple in Jerusalem; yet we are all from the heritage of our Father Abraham. Jesus had passed through this area many times, teaching Samaritans and Jews alike, so eventually I and others decided to settle here."

Jehosha pondered this information. "Then my heritage is the same as yours. I believe as you do, for my husband has led us to follow The Way of this area. In fact, my parents believe the same. We are raising our children as those who follow The Way."

She looked puzzled, then hesitant. "My father, please explain the difference between those who follow The Way, Pharisees and Sadducees. I have always been confused about this."

Jehosha had a quizzical look on her face as she watched her father-in-law stand and pace the room. "I do apologize for asking this question, but generally, my father, women are not allowed to ask such questions, but I know you will allow me to ask."

"Yes, I have no problem explaining it to you. Simply put, the difference, my daughter, is that the Sadducees, while being Jews, do not believe in the resurrection, nor do they believe in the existence of angels; whereas the Pharisees do and are publicly very vocal with their adherence to the Mosaic laws. Yet the Pharisees depend on the interpretation of the Law as written by the scribes."

"It seems the Sadducees are more strict concerning the Laws of Moses and what they believe to be its true interpretation. But too, they are very political and seem to agree with the political arena around them."

"Those who follow The Way follow the teachings of Jesus, believe in the resurrection, angels, and in treating others as ourselves in love."

"There is also a lot of conflict between the Pharisees and the Sadducees, for their separate beliefs are often at odds with each other even though the Sanhedrin is composed of both."

"You see, Jesus' focus was on the love of the Father and His kingdom. When Jesus was on this earth, He taught many things and I adhere to them, as well as my entire family." He smiled slowly as if remembering something Jesus said, and continued working the grapes. His fingers were very adept at working the tiny purple globes as he talked.

8

Still, Jehosha, wanted more information. "So how did you and Uzza court? And when did you marry? And how did you come to settle here?" Arushil took his seat once more and looked into her eyes.

"We did not court in the beginning because of Jewish restrictions, but Hezron had returned home a cleansed man and his family accepted him for his father was dead and he was the eldest son. They were happy to know that he was healed. They celebrated with family and friends as if he was a long-lost son. Hezron wanted me to attend his homecoming celebration also, but as soon as he explained to them I was a Samaritan, his family said no. Yet he would still come and visit with me."

"By that time I had returned to my home, but my family had moved elsewhere. Even my cousins had no idea of where they had gone. To this day, my family does not know that I have been healed. Another family was living in my old home, but they did not know where my family might be."

"When I walked through the orchards, I could see that some of the best grapevines had been clipped by my father and there were new seedlings as if the vines had been clipped at least five to six years ago. I could see that the new owners were not as well versed in vine-dressing as my family had been. Therefore, I requested if I would be allowed to clip some of the grapevines and they did not mind. Before I left, I explained how they could increase their crop of grapes by using pruning methods my father taught me."

"After clipping the vines, I took them with me to start up my own vineyards. My father was a great vine dresser and his grapes produced the finest wines in the valley. I remembered some of the ways he worked the grapes and copied his methods. This is why I am one of the best known winemakers in this area."

"The soil at my old home was good soil as well as here. Within a few years, my grapes had multiplied and Yahweh has blessed me to own all this land. Not bragging, but Uzza married a very well-to-do wine maker." He rubbed his beard as he chuckled.

"I would love to see my parents if they are still alive, for I also have a younger brother — my mother was pregnant when my boils began to show. My father would not let me near her in order to not mark the baby. To this day, no one really knows how this disease starts. I understood their reasoning, but even now, I would still like to see if any of my family is still alive. I can see them in my mind as at the age I left them to retreat to the hills."

"Before my healing, Uzza and I were able to become very close as we sat on different sides of Lepers Hill, for we thought alike. Then after my healing, we began to court. Her brother, Hezron knew and gave his blessing, for as the eldest son his blessing allowed us to be betrothed."

"After all, I was not poor; for as a maker of wine, which was my family's trade, my business grew. After our betrothal, which in the beginning was not approved by her parents, I moved here and continued my trade. By then, we were not just separated by distance, we were also separated by religious teachings.

"You see, Uzza's family are Pharisees and I had soon relocated to this valley, not knowing how close I actually was to her for Hezron's family had also moved near here. My cousins also follow Jesus' teachings and I and a few others who believe in His teachings, moved here. We are now accepted by both Pharisees and Sadducees even though we do not use their various synagogues."

"We also attend services here and it was at one of the services that Uzza and I were reunited. It was then that Hezron brought her to me on a Sabbath and we began courting in the traditional manner. We have a Levitical priesthood in the village. Uzza and I had our wedding in the synagogue in the square. The people who moved here helped to construct the small building, based on the Jerusalem Temple."

"There are people in this world who persecute those who follow The Way, but we are generally left alone in this area."

"Within a short period of time, Uzza's entire family accepted me — first as Hezron's friend, and then as Uzza's betrothed, and finally as in-law. We visit and communicate and they are beginning to follow The Way. Also, because of our close proximity, it gives her parents the chance to see their daughter Uzza, and their grandson and great-grandchildren." He chuckled once again at this last remark because he knew Joram's family would next be visiting with Uzza's family in a few weeks.

9

"But Opah," she reverted to the name the children called him, "what happened to Jesus the Teacher? You talk of Him as if in the past."

Arushil lowered his eyes. "He was killed years ago by the Roman death of crucifixion, but it was the Jews who really killed him." Slowly he related the death of a good man on the tree called the Roman cross at Golgotha and the exchanged release of a criminal named Barabbas.

"I was there when they killed Him – myself, Hezron, Ziljan, Jeconiah, and many others who had been healed by Him or who believed in His teachings. When we received word of His upcoming execution, we hurried to Jerusalem. The so-called religious Jews used false charges of heresy, blasphemy and other crimes, including accusations submitted by hired witnesses. Jesus only taught Yahweh's will for our lives, His love and peace for His people."

"He healed the sick, lame, demon-possessed and, of course, lepers. Whoever came to Him for healing was made well. Sometimes He laid hands on them and other times He just spoke healing on them. He was a good

Man, Jehosha, and your husband was raised by myself and Uzza in accordance with Jesus' teachings, which is why he, too, is a good man." Arushil smiled at this remark and Jehosha smilingly agreed.

"Jesus died Jehosha, but He has also been resurrected. He rose from the graves. He has been seen by many as well as by His disciples who have seen Him. His life and teachings live on."

"There are others of us who are known as the People of The Way. We meet in homes as well as in our small synagogue, and are free from the persecutions. More have joined us since the changing of royalty. Not many years ago, King Herod killed one of Jesus' disciples with the sword, which was followed by persecutions."

"Many are being slaughtered for believing in Jesus' teachings. There is a fear that Nero will become king and if he does so, who knows what will happen. The man is a raving lunatic and the People of The Way will have to be very careful."

"We of The Way have planned for a move in the event it looks as if persecutions will come toward us. We will move to the areas of Syria, Egypt, and other places. Not only will we spread the Good News or gospel, as it is known, of Jesus' teachings, for we know this movement will continue as He would want it."

Jehosha was confused. "Wait! How do you know this movement will continue?"

Arushil smiled. "It already has, my dear. Because I have told you that my son has lived under Jesus' teachings all his life, and now you and the children have been taught by my son and they are also being raised according to Jesus' teachings. And when they are older, they too will continue the teachings. We are to teach each other as well as all nations, which is what Jesus wanted us to do." Jehosha nodded her head in agreement.

10

"Now my daughter, it is time I finished my work in making the wine while it is still light and you must see to your children and husband. Thank you for listening and if you have more questions, both Uzza and I would be happy to give you answers." Arushil smiled warmly at his daughter-in-law and went back to straining the grapes for the new wine.

Jehosha stood and bent over to kiss the top of her father-in-law's head and gave his shoulders a loving squeeze. Heading toward the door, she looked back and saw Arushil still smiling after her. She raised one of her hands and gave a short wave, which he returned.

As she came out of the grape room, Jehosha met Uzza and Joram and all three smiled at each other. She put her hand out and Joram grabbed it and squeezed her fingers. Uzza picked up the baby, and placed the little girl on her hip.

The two small boys, running joyfully, followed behind them as they traveled back toward the main part of the house.

BETHZATHA

THE HEALING
AT THE POOL

**A Fictional Story Using Scripture
From the Book of St. John 5:1-14**

HISTORICAL FACTS ON THE POOL OF BETHZATHA

In some manuscripts, this Pool in Jerusalem was called **Bethzatha** or **Bethsaida** *("House of Mercy"* or *"House of Healing")*. Most Christians know it as **Bethesda** from the King James translation. One belief is that the Hebrews felt the water's movement came from angels sent by God to stir it up – possibly by the movement of their wings. However, there is no reference to angels or angels' wings stirring the waters in the Roman or Greek manuscripts. There is also another belief that God Himself would blow His breath on the waters causing rippling waves with healing powers to heal those who were first able to get into the water. Whoever gets into the pool either during or after the start of each rippling would be cured of their disease or infirmity.

Bethzatha was once outside the city of Jerusalem, but during the rule of Herod the Great, a northern wall was added to Jerusalem prior to the birth of Christ, incorporating the Pool with a pipeline leading to it. The water would rush daily through the pipes, keeping the water somewhat clear. Yet, it was also reported that there were times the water would not be always clear in the afternoon, having a murky reddish or brown color at various times in late afternoon or evening, perhaps caused by the setting sun's reflection on the water.

This Pool was considered to be very beautiful, having five large colonnades with porches. In the middle section, the sick and infirm were allowed to congregate. It was inlaid with marble and stone, surrounded by sculptures of granite with gold edging placed along its sides.

Nehemiah 3:1 reports the Sheep Gate was built on the authority of the High Priest Eliashib. The priestly staff at that time built and sanctified the gate, its doors and the surrounding area following its rebuilding, which made the entire area Holy.

In this story of healing at the Pool of Bethzatha (or Bethesda, as it is commonly known), the main character, Shimron, had been infirmed for decades. What was his sin? Was he informed for a reason?

Biblically, the man was told to "go and sin no more." He must have been able to walk at some time, for the Bible does not say he was infirmed since birth, but for nearly 40 years. I placed Shimron's age to be at least 55 or 60 at the time of this story. His sin was not given in scripture, so I used the sin of spreading gossip or lying.

History relates that many of the people begging alms outside the Temple and synagogues were known to listen to the conversations of people who entered and exited or who were nearby. Those who sat by the gates and doors had privy to many conversations and since they had nothing else to do, were prone to repeat what they believed they overheard. Sometimes if the gossip was juicy to others, the information could be sold for a few coins. The juicier the story, the more coins the invalid might receive.

The Pool was considered sacred, not just because of the movement of the water, but because of its sacred dedication by the priests during Nehemiah's time, as well as its close proximity to the Temple.

BETHZATHA

He mumbled as he prepared himself for the new day. It was almost the Sabbath and soon no work could be done. "Those young so-called scribes are always trying to see if I'm going to be late. They know I have to be there early or I won't be able to get a good spot."

Shimron was angry because the Temple priests, in trying to be helpful, would give him another scribe each month. This time his scribe helper was Zendor, one of the new trainees to help him. "They gave that scribe to me probably because no one else wanted to be bothered with me," he thought to himself.

Shimron could always find someone to take him to the Temple in the center of Jerusalem because he knew people would make their way there two to three times a day and they would do anything for money, even cart him back and forth. So someone would help him get to his regular spot beside the Temple doors each morning, and he could always pay someone else to cart him back to his small hovel. Shimron's alms helped to pay the people who carried him back and forth and the men who helped him always accepted his money. Most of the men who carted him back and forth did not like him but would take his money nonetheless.

"Jerusalem, Holy City, City of God, bah! A city with a bunch of priests, scribes and hypocrites if you ask me," he grumbled.

But Shimron had a major fault -- he was a gossip and rumormonger, and if he didn't have all the facts, he would make something up and add more interesting parts to his news. The townspeople became aware of Shimron's stories when their personal business became a part of his rumors and discussions. Many did not mind listening to some of his stories until their names or their friends' names were used in his fabrications, and eventually the worshippers complained to the priests.

The priests then suggested to Shimron that perhaps it would be incumbent for him to get to the Pool at Bethzatha at a good time each morning and perhaps receive a healing. They did not want him sitting on his pallet outside the Temple begging alms while listening to the conversations of those coming and going.

When told of the change, Shimron used the excuse that he could not get to the Pool because it was by the Sheep Gate which was located north of the Temple and no one would take him there. In Shimron's mind was also the fact that if he did not get his healing at the Pool, he would lose his revenue from begging alms, for very few people contributed alms to the people by the Pool.

The High Priest's idea was to give him a "trainee" scribe to make sure Shimron reached the Bethzatha Pool and situate him in an area close to the water before the designated scribe reported to his duties in the Temple. Therefore, new scribes were each given a month to work with Shimron, and this month the scribe to transport him was a shy young man named Zendor.

Zendor was young, muscular, pleasant and highly biddable, and they knew he would be able to put up with Shimron's grumblings. The other scribes complained about dragging the infirmed man and his belongings on the short cot – they complained that Shimron was heavy, had too much stuff to carry, had an odor, and constantly insulted them as if it was their fault he was unable to walk.

They also reported back to the priests some of the rumors and gossip that Shimron was spreading. Since Zendor was not a complainer and refused to listen to Shimron's stories, he was not overly happy with the scribe.

His thoughts went back to the first day he met Zendor. The young man had knocked on his window and bowed low as he introduced himself. He was well dressed and he could see that the young man's beard was new growth. Unlike the other scribes, Zendor brought a long flat wagon with wheels instead of the cot to place Shimron's belongings on, and there was ample room for Shimron to sit. Shimron had to admit that sitting on the wagon was much more comfortable than the scribes dragging him on the cot across the bumpy ground.

Shimron crawled toward the window and saw he was not late. The break of day was just starting as he placed his food on the table. The scribe would soon come knocking at his door. "I must hurry," he thought, "for if I'm late Zendor will probably use that as an excuse and leave me behind." Zendor had never done this, but the other scribes had left him twice with the excuse that they could not be late in getting him to the Pool.

Shimron failed to realize that these new scribes could not be late reporting for their duties at the Temple, for they could be chastised by the priests. After all, their first duty was to the Temple and Zendor knew today was the Sabbath and the scribes were required to be on time.

Shimron placed his pallet, two wooden sticks he used as canes, the day's food, and a pillow beside the door. Soon, he was hurriedly opening the door to young Zendor's knock. "Good morning Shimron; are you ready?" Zendor gave him a broad smile as he brought the wagon into the house and quickly began piling Shimron's belongings onto it.

"Let's get going before the sun actually rises for today is the Sabbath. The faster we get there, the closer you'll be able to sit by the water. By the way, I have already picked out a nice area to the right of the Pool and placed some items there to hold your spot."

Zendor was astute and knew the reason he was given to Shimron for all the scribes had discussed it. The older man had been infirm for over thirty-eight years, and was considered Jerusalem's main gossip in the city. Shimron could spread a rumor within an hour of hearing it, listening to anything he felt might be news to tell others, whether true or false. His gossip had hurt men, women, children, priests and officials.

But, of course, since Shimron was on his pallet daily beside the Temple, begging alms and had no friends to speak of, Zendor realized he had nothing else to do except listen to whatever conversations were nearby. Sometimes he took pity on Shimron's plight, but he also dreaded his duty to the grumbling old man.

This month was Zendor's month to pick up Shimron in the mornings, place him and his belongings on the cot and drag him to the Pool. He figured being bounced along the road on the flat cot to their destination could have been part of the reason Shimron complained so much.

He discussed the matter with his older brother, Tahan-Makir. To help his brother and to make the infirmed man more comfortable, Tahan-Makir constructed a flat wagon with small wheels on the bottom, and added pieces of soft fur to the seating area to take the older man and his belongings to be deposited near the Pool. Another scribe would bring Shimron home the same way and place the wagon by his door in readiness for the next day.

Zendor's monthly duty was almost completed and he could not be happier; for he was being promoted and moved to another area of the Temple where he would be able to do more of the Lord's work.

In no time, they had reached the Pool. Many infirmed, blind, mute and crippled people were already there. He saw a few new crippled persons and realized the area was becoming much more crowded. The spot Zendor had picked was the closest he had ever been to the Pool. The scribe began removing Shimron's items and placed them on the marbled tile.

He finished his duty and patted Shimron on the back as he moved toward the arch that exited the area. "Have a pleasant day, Shimron, and I'm praying you get into the water first when the movement begins!" Waving, he left the area as Shimron grumbled, "Oh sure, only if the water begins to move while I'm trying to get there." The men and women around the pool ignored the cantankerous older man as he scooted a bit closer to the edge.

Bethzatha was a beautiful Pool. It was not like the Roman baths where men would sometimes jump into the pool and swim and splash around like children as they bathed. No one swam in Bethzatha.

People were camped around about the porticos waiting for the movement of the waters. Bethzatha was not very deep and the water came down from the high mountains on the outskirts of Jerusalem. No one knew how it happens, but every once in a while, the waters would seem to ripple, bubble and boil, but not become hot. Some said an angel would come down and move the waters, but no one had ever seen the angel. Others said God would blow His breath to make the water ripple. The first person to get into the waters when it did so was immediately healed.

There were five porches or colonnades around it filled with people who awaited healing. Shimron was a part of the people known as the "unallowed ones" of the city. These people were not allowed in the Temple because they were imperfect—they were the lame, crippled, blind and withered people. The only ones not allowed near the Pool were the lepers. They had to constantly stay in areas outside Jerusalem for they were the "unclean" ones because of their disease.

This day was very special as the Jews had been celebrating a special holy feast and it was also the Sabbath. There had been food and special markets and celebrations for the past couple of days. Many Jews from other areas were there to celebrate, as well as Gentile travelers from afar and hordes of tradesmen from around the Roman Empire and beyond who came to sell their wares.

The water had not moved for many days and all were hoping there would be movement of the waters today – or tomorrow – or the next day. Hope made the unallowed ones come every day. Some stayed overnight in one spot for if they moved from their area, another infirmed person might move into their space and they would miss their healing.

Many of them died waiting for their chance to get into the Pool. When this happened someone else would move into the empty place. Shimron praised God that Zendor had picked this spot for him for it was very close.

"That young man just might be good for something after all," he mumbled to himself.

A young man about the age of 30 or so walked through one of the porticos and quietly passed by. As he did so, he hesitated when he spotted Shimron. The man could see that Shimron and the others around the Pool had various physical problems, but it seemed as if he set his sights on him and stared at the older man.

Shimron could feel his eyes upon him, so he finally turned and stared back. Yet, there was compassion in his face, not the pity normally shown by the city's citizens. The man came closer and Shimron thought he was probably guessing he had been infirm for many years.

At first Shimron thought, "What's he looking at? Has he never seen a deformed man before?" Slowly Shimron averted his eyes and looked instead toward the water in the Pool. He must have blinked too long for when he turned around the man was almost beside him looking at his legs, pallet and bundles.

"Do you want to get well? Would you like to be made whole?" the Man asked. Shimron thought to himself, "Why ask such questions? He's not giving me any money. Can't he see me sitting here waiting to get well?"

Shimron then began to whine. "Sir, I don't have anyone to help me into the pool when it ripples. Every time I try to get to the edge so I can get in, someone beats me to it. Someone else always goes into the Pool ahead of me.

I don't have anyone who can help me quickly get there." He then held out his hands in the event the man wanted to give him a few coins.

The Man locked eyes with Shimron and said in a commanding voice, "Get up! Pick up your pallet and walk!"

Immediately, Shimron felt strength in his body and his legs began to tingle as he watched them straighten. Slowly he moved into a crawling position then wobbled a bit as he arose, and realized he was soon able to stand on his own. He began to rejoice for he knew he was healed. He could stand! He could walk! It had been so long!

Reaching down, he did as he was told and picked up his pallet, rolled it and tucked it under his arm. Leaving his other belongings, he began walking around the Pool and praising God. The people around the Pool watched as he began to slowly walk, then skip around the statues. He headed toward one of the columns and held the side, breathing heavy while still rejoicing. He then lost sight of the man who told him to get up.

He soon left the Pool area and headed for the arch to leave. His first thought was to see if he could walk all the way back home. Still rejoicing, he headed for his house.

Many of the Jews saw him walking with his pallet under his arm and murmured among themselves, "Doesn't he know this is the Sabbath? He shouldn't be carrying anything! Not only that, isn't this the man who has been lying beside the Temple doors begging alms?"

Others remembered him and some mentioned how his legs used to be crooked and had seen him at the Pool of Bethzatha awaiting healing. Had he experienced the rippling of the waters? Shimron didn't care what was said and, still rejoicing, continued on his way. Some even followed him as he headed toward his home.

Eventually three high-ranking Jews caught up with him and asked why he was carrying a burden on the Sabbath. "Don't you know that the Law of Moses states that there would be no work, or carrying of any items on this day?" They looked upon Shimron with disdain.

"Yes," he answered, "but the man who healed me said I should pick up my pallet and walk. I am going home now to clean up and bring two birds to sacrifice for my healing. I want to show myself to the priests so that I may now go into the Temple."

"Man, what man? Who healed you?" They questioned Shimron further, but he had no answer for them. "I only know that when I got up from my pallet my legs and body had gained strength and I could walk. By the time I looked up, the man was gone. I only know he must have been a man truly sent from God!"

Shimron bowed to them and hurried home to clean himself. He pulled out his old chest, reached in and found good clothing, and began putting on clothes he had not worn in almost 38 or 39 years. And, strangely, they fit!

He used some of his alms and stopped to purchase two doves for sacrifice before heading to present himself to the priests. He began skipping and twirling himself as he headed for the priests area to show he was cleansed of his infirmity.

He was happy and realized this was not only the Sabbath, but a feast day. What a day to be healed! Before, one day was as another. Since he was only allowed in the outer courts, but not inside the Temple, he never felt like celebrating – until today.

As he was leaving the priests area following the atonement sacrifice for his healing, the Man who healed him met him in one of the Temple hallways. Some of the people were following Him and he heard them call the man "Jesus" and "Rabbi."

When he used to sit by the Temple doors, Shimron had heard of this Jesus and how he had healed in many of the areas around Galilee and Judea. Jesus called to him and Shimron went to him smiling broadly.

"I am healed, my Lord! I am healed," he cried as with his arms outstretched, he turned in a circle to show Jesus. He was so happy as he bowed and stretched in front of Jesus.

Jesus returned his smile but began to quietly admonish him, "Yes, you are made whole. But you are to stop sinning or something worse will happen to you."

At first Shimron thought, "I have not sinned. How can a man sin if he cannot move because of his infirmities?" But then he realized how he loved to gossip and spread rumors. He had a sinful tongue. It was time to make amends to some of the people for the lies and gossip he'd told concerning them; many had been hurt by his words. He did not want to go back into the same condition or anything worse that could happen as Jesus said. If Jesus knew of this, then he had a lot of apologizing to do.

First, he wanted to find Zendor and apologize to him as well as some of the other scribes whose feelings he may have hurt.

As he was leaving the Temple area, he ran into the same three Jews who had previously questioned him about the man who healed him. Shimron was happy to explain to them he was healed by Jesus the Teacher and told them the entire story of how he was at the Pool and how Jesus stopped to speak with him. He also mentioned that Jesus told him he needed to stop sinning.

"You know, Jesus asked me a question, and instead of answering it, I began mumbling and complaining. He asked if I wanted to be healed and I never said 'yes'." Shimron was contrite for a few seconds and then said, "He knew I wanted to be made well. He knew, and he healed me right then."

Knowing he had things to make right, Shimron bowed before the men and said that if he had hurt any of them with his words, he wanted to apologize. The men looked at him as if he was deranged and politely accepted his apology.

Shimron went on his way to find the area where the Temple scribes were situated, and as he left, the three men turned back toward the Temple to tell the High Priest about Jesus healing people on the Sabbath.

The Temple doorkeepers halted Shimron at the front arch as he approached them. "I am looking for the area or rooms of the scribes for I need to talk to the trainees." The doorkeepers looked as if they would not allow him to go any further, but Shimron argued he must find the scribes. Hearing a disturbance in the hallway, Zendor and a few other scribes poked their heads out of a room toward the rear.

They were surprised to see Shimron standing and talking with the doorkeepers, laughing and raising his arms. They came to the front and told the doorkeepers they knew him. Pulling Shimron by his arm, they led him to one of the hallway's stone seats. All began talking at the same time, sounding like a chattering bunch of monkeys.

"What happened? Is it you, Shimron? How are you walking? Have you been fooling us all this time? Did the waters move? Were you healed at Bethzatha?" Shimron told them of his healing and how Jesus told him not to sin any more.

"I wanted to come here to apologize for how I have treated you when you've all been helpful to me. Please let me ask your forgiveness." All nodded their heads. Then, turning to Zendor, he apologized profusely.

"Zendor, you and your brother, Tahan-Makir, gave me the wagon to make me more comfortable. And you put me in a place where Jesus could get to me by the Pool at Bethzatha. I most humbly apologize and thank you. Because of all of you, I am now able to worship inside the Temple, not only for services, but also for feast days! I apologize to you all. I am leaving now to find Jesus, so that I may know more about Him."

For another year Shimron became a follower of Jesus and when others would dispute his healing, he would direct them to the scribes in the Temple. Zendor and the other scribes could honestly tell others how Shimron had been one of the infirmed at the Pool of Bethzatha and how they carried him there daily.

Shimron no longer gossiped or made up stories and over time people began to trust him and believed he was a miracle caused by the healing of Jesus the Christ.

EPILOGUE

It was now a few years after his healing by Jesus. Shimron sat beside his door with his head down. He had become a follower and witness of Jesus the Healer. Whenever he could get anyone to listen, he would tell of his healing and how he had been infirm for almost 40 years. If Jesus was in the area, whenever Jesus taught or led in ministry, he was always in attendance. He believed Jesus was the Messiah and enjoyed being around Him.

Yet, just a few weeks ago, the Sanhedrin and priests had crucified Jesus on the outskirts of Jerusalem. Although it was a Roman death sentence, Shimron knew it was the Pharisees and Sadducees who had him killed. He tried to follow Jesus as he left the city to travel the road to Golgotha, but the crush of the crowd held him back.

He had watched as a dark-skinned Cyrenian man was pulled from the crowd by the soldiers and ordered to finish carrying Jesus' crucifix up the hill. The Romans saw Jesus was too weak to carry it and made the man lift the wood from Jesus' weak arms and continue carrying it. Was this an act of compassion on the part of the soldiers, or only a move to complete the task of crucifying the Man as quickly as possible?

In the distance Shimron had seen the grieving family of the Healer and mourned with them. The mother was weeping so hard that he began to weep along with her. Even Pilate did not believe Jesus was guilty of heresy, treason or any other crime.

And where were Jesus' followers? There were always a dozen or so men with him when he traveled through Jerusalem and its outskirts, but only one of his disciples was at the foot of the crucifixion tree. What was his name? John! Yes, that was his name. John was sorrowing beside Jesus' mother during the crucifixion. How she must have cried out as they hammered each nail into his limbs!

Strange happenings had taken place during and following the crucifixion: The sacred curtains in the Temple had been ripped from the bottom up. For the first time, many saw what was behind the sacred curtains known as the Holy of Holies. The sky had darkened as if God Himself was angry at what was taking place. Others claimed to have seen people who had died walking the streets. There had been a horrible earthquake and houses were tumbled to the ground while parts of the city's earth cracked open.

He was told that following Jesus' death on the tree, some prominent Jews had requested of Pilate the body of Jesus and they were given permission. It was rumored they might be part of the same Sanhedrin that had pushed for Him to be crucified. After Jesus' death, they took His body from the crucifixion tree and placed it in one of their tombs.

The Sanhedrin wanted to have Roman guards placed around the tomb and permission was given. Now it is said that Jesus arose from the dead and walked away from the tomb.

The Sanhedrin, consisting of Pharisees and Sadducees, seemed to be in agreement for once. Generally there was dissension among them, for each sect had their own agenda. Yet, they were together in plotting Jesus' death — even to the point of putting silver together to give to a greedy man named Judas of Iscariot who was instrumental in bringing the Healer to trial. What was strange was the fact that this man was one of the 12 who traveled with Him. There were those who said Judas tried to return the money, but the Sanhedrin would not take it for it was now 'blood money.'

This Judas later hanged himself near a cliff. Rumor has it that he didn't do the deed correctly for his body fell off the tree and was later found splattered near the cliff's edge. A field was purchased with the silver he had been paid, and his body was buried there.

Shimron had met with a few of the Roman guards who were sent to guard the tomb. They swore they were struck dumb when a powerful unseen force opened the tomb by rolling the stone aside. That talk was quickly hushed, and it is believed they were paid by members of the Sanhedrin to not broadcast that story. The guards were told to tell anyone who asked that someone else brought strong men to open the tomb. Members of the Sanhedrin, especially the Sadducees, did not want it spread that a dead man had walked out of the tomb on his own.

There was also talk of angels being near the tomb, but the Sadducees, who did not believe in angels or resurrections, denounced that story. Supposedly Jesus had been seen by some of the area's women as well as many of Jesus' disciples. The Pharisees and the Sadducees believed they must have been the ones who helped to open the tomb and had the body carried away.

* * *

Shimron lifted his head upon hearing voices of two men as they traveled toward his house. Hardly anyone came his way for he lived on the outskirts of the city and the road only led to Emmaus, which was about 11 kilometers away. The two men were excitedly talking about traveling with the risen Jesus and breaking bread with Him.

Shimron got up from his stool and followed them at a safe distance to listen to their conversation. Wanting to hear more, he called out to the men to wait for him. They stopped and waited as he joined them. They said they were heading back to Jerusalem and told how they had previously met with Jesus' disciples and joyously told the story to some of them and about their fellowship with the Lord. Shimron continued with them as they headed toward Jerusalem with all three talking excitedly.

As the three headed toward the city, Shimron told of his healing. Then the two men related stories to Shimron how Jesus had healed the sick, lame and blind, even lepers and the demon-possessed. Both men excitedly explained that Jesus was alive and related how they had walked and talked with Him on this very road.

"He has risen, just as he said," they announced to Shimron. "Jesus is not dead, He lives! It is true, for we are witnesses!"

Silently crying, Shimron lifted his hands in praise. "He's alive!" he whispered to himself. "He is truly alive!"

He listened as the men told how Jesus had prophesized that He would be killed and in three days would rise from the dead.

"Jesus had said the Temple would be raised again in three days. He was really talking about Himself for Jesus was the Temple! He did not mean the building in Jerusalem—He was speaking of Himself as the Temple. And what Jesus had said came true."

That is just what He did, Shimron thought, the Temple was raised!

Until his death, instead of gossip, Shimron would repeat his testimony to anyone who would listen, and as he finished his story, he would always end it with Jesus' resurrection. Shimron said it was his job to tell others about his healing, for he knew he was meant to be a witness to all who had no hope.

Lonnie-Sharon Williams is a graduate of Cleveland State University and a retired middle school teacher. Prior to teaching, she was a paralegal-secretary at major law firms in Cleveland. She has been the recipient of many grants and awards in the teaching and legal fields. Ms. Williams is a biblical history buff and has been writing short stories, skits and poems since the age of 10. This is her first published work, with another almost completed.

Ms. Williams has one adult son, Robert and daughter-in-law Clare, and loves to attend concerts and plays. She loves to listen to all forms of music and performs as a character actor and liturgical dancer. She and her cat, Mykal, reside in Cleveland.